TRY NOT TO DIE

In

This Damned House

ROBERT ESSIG

VINCERE
PRESS

Published by Vincere Press
65 Pine Ave., Ste 806
Long Beach, CA 90802

Try Not to Die: In This Damned House

Printed in the United States of America
First Edition

ISBN: 9781961740297
Library of Congress Control Number: 2024921985

Front and back cover by Jun Ares
Edit by Mark Tullius and Horrorsmith Editing

An Important Note from the Publisher

After reading Robert Essig's *This Damned House*, I asked him if he'd be interested in creating a *Try Not to Die* (TNTD) book. I didn't give him any restrictions, trusting that whatever he delivered would surprise me in the best way. Some of the images and scenes from his past work have stayed with me, so I knew this new project would do the same—and I was right.

It's with mixed excitement and trepidation that I present this book as the first *extreme* TNTD title. I won't lie—this one makes me uncomfortable. I've never been one for horror that pushes too far into the extreme, and while I can handle a bit of death and gore, the genre often crosses boundaries I'm reluctant to approach. But when I read this manuscript, I found myself disturbed in the best possible way—so compelled to keep going, even as I cringed at some of the darker, more graphic scenes.

We briefly considered removing the most intense material, but ultimately, I decided to leave it in, with this warning and a list of triggers on the next page. Just because I'm not comfortable with certain things doesn't mean others will feel the same way, and I want to respect that.

This book marks a few firsts for the *Try Not to Die* series. Not only is it the first extreme entry, but it also features adult characters grappling with adult problems. The structure itself is also unique, echoing the format of Essig's *This Damned House* with four distinct stories.

So, if you're ready for a deeply disturbing journey, go ahead and turn the page. But be warned: the odds are stacked against you. Don't expect an easy ride. Prepare to suffer. And yes, you will die.

Mark Tullius

If you want to familiarize yourself with both *Damned Houses*, you can find them where books are sold.

This Damned House

and

This Damned House II

Trigger Warning

As mentioned in my note, this book delves into extreme horror and contains numerous intense and potentially disturbing themes. While the following list covers many of the most prominent triggers, please be aware that it may not capture everything. Please read with caution.

For those who wish to experience the book but avoid the most graphic content, I recommend stopping after the third short story, *Afterimage*.

Content Warning Includes:

- Sexual Assault
- Physical, Emotional, and Psychological Abuse
- Child Abuse and Death
- Self-Harm and Suicide
- Miscarriage/Abortion
- Alcohol Abuse and Addiction
- Amputation and Mutilation
- Forced Captivity and Kidnapping
- Mental Illness
- Necrophilia

Please proceed with care and know that your well-being is important.

TRY NOT TO DIE
In This Damned House

Markus's time in the attic was a seemingly never-ending source of amusement, watching the town of Greenwood Planes through his telescope. People were fascinating, especially so when he manipulated them. The best part was, his manipulations were only the beginning. The end results were a surprise, even to him.

In the center of the attic was a large table with a scale model of Greenwood Planes. It had been there for decades. Built by his grandfather for the sole purpose, Markus surmised, of exploiting the townsfolk. Perhaps it was in the blood. Perhaps he was a magic man. Whatever the reason, Markus discovered his talents very young, before his parents drank themselves into oblivion and inevitably succumbed to their vices.

Markus sensed a kinship with his grandfather he'd never shared with either his father or mother. They were not like him. Maybe the magic skipped a generation. Maybe Father couldn't do what he and ol' Grandpa could.

Markus stood over the model of Greenwood Planes and scanned the buildings, deciding which he would torment next. He just built two more in place of the mess he made of the previous structures. It was a lot of fun watching the tenants lose their minds and kill one another. And that one unit with the roaches...yikes! The thought of it gave Markus the willies.

He decided on an apartment. A fourplex. Those were his favorite to exercise his devious talents. He'd done a number on a single-family dwelling but found something unsatisfactory about it. There was an added tension with unusual activities in a building shared by multiple people.

Now the only question was, what would he place inside the first window? That was the key to kicking off what would prove to be a fatal encounter for the tenant. At least, they had all been fatal up to this point. Markus was not aware of any strict rules or guidelines when it came to the magic of the model of Greenwood Planes. All he knew was, it worked.

On a TV tray beside his favorite chair, where he would sit and watch the town endlessly through his telescope, was a plate of scraps from lunch. Or was it dinner? A few bean sprouts from his sandwich lay there like errant hairs. He grinned, shrugged, and plucked them from the plate, placing them into a window of his chosen fourplex apartment.

It wouldn't take long for things to shake up in that unit. What kind of damage could a few sprouts do?

Markus sat in his chair, spying on the apartment through his telescope and thinking about his legacy. He'd continued what his grandfather started, but who would be there to continue *his* work? Was it even so important for Markus to concern himself with legacy?

He had no children, not so much as a love interest. Markus didn't even know how to speak to women. He hardly knew how to communicate with anyone, being his life had been one of seclusion, in the house upon the hill overlooking a town his grandfather built from the ground up. A town Markus continued to build and rebuild, over and over again.

He watched the couple in the unit he'd placed the sprouts in only minutes ago, but he was thinking about who would take his place when he was gone.

Pieces of Me

It's just after the evening news when I find the first sprout on my body. I think it's an errant hair at first, one of those stubborn, thick hairs which typically grows from a large mole. The type that is very painful when plucked. But it is merely a sprout, and though I should maybe be more curious about where the damn thing came from, I pinch it between thumb and forefinger and yank it off my arm, figuring it became plastered there by a gluing of dried mayo from lunch.

Problem is, I didn't have a sandwich with sprouts on it, nor did I have a salad. So where did the damn thing come from?

A tiny prick pinches my skin when it is extracted. I examine the little sprout, its miniscule stem white with a small pair of pale green leaves. A dot of blood lingers where the roots dangle like miniature optic nerves.

Something about it disgusts me. I rub the tiny sprout into oblivion between my fingers and wipe the remnants onto a tissue.

"Honey?" I holler from my perch on the couch, then wait patiently for Tanya to reply.

The apartment isn't all that big. She has to have heard me. Once I sit down after work, I am reluctant to get up for much of anything outside of dinner and taking a leak.

"Honey, I wanna ask you something." I holler louder this time. Hopefully, she hears me. I swear, if I have to get up—

"Gary, just a minute." Her voice comes swiftly from somewhere in the apartment.

I sigh. What is she doing that is so important she can't come out here and answer me one simple question?

I scratch my arm where the sprout was and return my gaze to the television. After the news, I settled on reruns of *Seinfeld*. I don't know how many times I've watched this show, but somehow, it never gets old.

Finally, her footfalls thump down the hallway. I have been in a pretty good mood, all things considered, but something about her steps drives me up the wall. She is annoyed with me, putting extra emphasis on each dull thud of her foot on the hardwood floor—an auditory warning, like the rattling tale of a venomous snake.

"What is it, Gary?" She has folds of foil in her hair and is wearing one of those old T-shirts with stains and holes on it, reserved strictly for chores such as painting, cleaning, or hair dye.

"Did I interrupt something?" I ask.

Tanya rolls her eyes, sighs, and balls her fists against her hips. Yep, she is irritated for sure. I heard her footfalls correctly, her death rattle shakes. God forbid I have a simple question.

"I'm in the middle of doing my hair."

I nod. At fifty-three, you'd think she'd be done with all this dying her hair radical colors, but I married a woman who can't stick with one style.

"What color are you putting in your hair now?"

"Just highlights." Tanya shrugs and extends her hands, palms up, in a who-cares gesture. "So, what do you want? I need to finish."

"You buy sprouts recently?"

She looks at me like I'm a madman. "What?"

"You know, sprouts like for salads and sandwiches."

"What kind of question is that?" Tanya shakes her head. "No, I haven't bought sprouts in a long time. Do you know how much sprouts are? We can't afford that on your paycheck."

"Oh."

Then where the fuck did it come from?

"You know, you're really losing it, Gary. I swear to God, you ask me the stupidest questions sometimes."

Tanya walks away, thumping down the hall in an aggressive manner which says more than words. She closes the bathroom door with something close to a slam, and I wonder how it is we cannot afford groceries and yet she buys hair dye.

*****

Keep my mouth shut. Turn to page 8.

Confront Tanya about buying hair dye when you can't afford it. Turn to page 80.

"There's no need for that," I say in a raised voice, stopping Jan before she can swing her blessed hunk of sharpened steel into Danny's head.

Jan's eyes are fire. "Then get him in line right now! Time's a-wasting."

He continues to freak out.

"Calm down, Danny," I say, in what I hope is a reassuring tone. I try to look him in the eyes, but he's crying and frantic. "It's going to be all right."

He shakes his head. "No! Nothing is going to be all right. Why do people always say that, even though they *know* nothing will be all right?"

Danny bolts for the front door. Jan is after him like a hawk on a field mouse. I have no time to block her advance before the cleaver slices into Danny's back. He yelps and goes down, hitting his head against the front door when he falls. The sound is so loud, the neighbors must hear.

The blade is stuck in his spinal column. He doesn't move, probably paralyzed.

I, too, am immobilized with fear and shock, an avalanche of thoughts, a torrent of regrets, a tidal wave of forgiveness. It all hits me then, all so unexpected, as if I somehow am accepting the fact this is my end. It's like I'm rooted to the floor.

I snap out of this bizarre daze and move to act, but Jan has her hands on the cleaver. She yanks it out of Danny's back. His screams are nothing but agony, though his body remains still, further assuring me he is paralyzed.

Jan swings the cleaver toward me, and I am again taken aback by her agility for a woman her age. The way she leapt after Danny was almost cat-like.

"Look what you did!" she yells. "Now there's more mess to clean up. I don't have time for this shit! I really don't. The ladies will be here at five sharp, and I have a*nother* body to contend with. And all because of you!"

"Me?"

"Yes, you. Clearly, I hired the wrong company for this job."

"This is crazy. *You're* crazy!"

Something comes over me, and I press forward, bringing fists to a cleaver fight. This is a mistake. She swings the blade, making contact with my wrist and hacking off my hand in one clean swipe. It is so unexpected and quick, I am left in shock. There isn't even pain. I hold the stump before me and watch blood squirt straight up.

"Good god, you're getting it all over the ceiling," she says. "How am I ever going to clean *that*?"

I then position my squirting stump toward Jan, trying to get her in the eyes, but she's quick and ducks my strange defense, lumbering toward me like she's going to tackle me to the ground. She swings her precious cleaver into my chest. The blade hits me like being punched, only there is a bite to the impact. The blade slices through flesh and muscle and becomes embedded in my ribs.

I go down, landing hard on the floor amidst the blood of both Thomas and Danny Boy.

"You goddamn asshole." She pulls the cleaver free.

All this fight catches up to Jan, and she takes heavy breaths before bringing the cleaver down into my flesh again.

"You'll never get this all cleaned in time." I choke out those final words with a small geyser of bloody spittle.

She hacks and hacks. It hurts.

I scream.

***

Try again. Turn to page 51.

Our relationship hasn't always been so strained. People don't fall in love like that. Had we met one another with the attitudes we throw around these days, we wouldn't have so much as gone on a first date. It takes time and effort to become so bitter—two people who slowly grow apart but still feel a closeness keeping them together. It's complicated but seems to work for us.

I'm a fairly patient man and keep a lot of my feelings to myself concerning Tanya. But I'm sure she hears the sighs and grumbling beneath my breath when I've had it up to here. Isn't that the way older married couples are with one another?

That's what I always thought, but Tanya likes to point out other couples and compare us, as if I'm a scumbag for not holding her hand in public or giving her flowers. I always tell her not to live vicariously through social media, where people only play a highlights reel of a life probably very similar to ours, but she doesn't listen to me.

Things get stale. The nine-to-five beats me down. By the time I get home, I'm exhausted. My comfy chair calls to me, and I sit down in the spot perfectly shaped to my undercarriage. I have a beer and watch the news, and I'm content with this. Tanya, on the other hand, is not, and she's vocal about it.

I guess you could say we're *that* old married couple.

It is the following morning, while I prepare myself for work, that I see the next sprouts.

Hands coated in shaving cream, I am about to give myself the ol' Santa Claus face lathering when I notice the strange growth on my cheek. I stare into the mirror in shock, wash the white from my paws, and flick one of the sprouts with my finger. It has grown from the flesh of my cheek.

"What the holy hell is going on?" I ask my reflection.

I grab one of the sprouts and pull gently, but it seems to be rooted deep. While I tug, the flesh pulls like I'm grabbing a hair, and then the intruder finally comes free. The pinch comes again, only this time, a tiny dot of red appears where the sprout is extracted. The roots are red as well.

I level my gaze upon the other foreign growth and stare for a moment. Crazy thoughts flash in my mind. I pluck it in one quick motion and wash them both down the drain, then shave my face before heading off to work.

Only, I don't go to work. I begin to feel ill.

Back in the day, I would just go to work when I felt under the weather, but these days, I've learned it is better to take a few PTO days and get well before putting more stress on my body. People are still concerned with Covid anyway. Better to take a day or two off than worry my coworkers.

I stand in the kitchen with a hot cup of coffee, hearing something down the hall. Outside of the occasional footsteps from the neighbors above, it is a typical quiet morning. I crane my head out the kitchen door and into the hall to listen.

The sound is faint but seems to be coming from our bedroom, where Tanya is still sleeping. I listen closely, trying to distinguish what I am hearing. Has she turned the television on inside our bedroom? It wouldn't be like her to wake up and immediately turn on the TV like that. Not without using the bathroom and getting some coffee first. And even then, I would assume she would watch TV in the living room, if she felt so inclined. The weird part is, I can't quite distinguish the language. It is like someone chanting gibberish.

Is she talking in her sleep?

When I near the bedroom door, the chanting takes on an eerie quality, reminding me of something specific. And yet, I can't put my finger on it. I step closer, listening intently, when my foot hits a soft spot on the floor that creaks.

The strange voice halts.

I stand there as if paralyzed, waiting for it to return. The hallway is engulfed in silence. I decide to open the door and ask what it is I heard. Only, when I push the door open, the hinges whaling in protest, Tanya is fast asleep in bed. The steady rhythm of her heavy breathing is a certain indicator she has been asleep the entire time.

I creep out of the bedroom, gently close the door behind me, and pad down the hall toward the living room. At the other end of the apartment, I sit in my comfy chair and turn on the morning news. I sip my coffee and watch the talking heads pontificate on the same tired stories they hashed through yesterday evening.

The strange chanting I heard remains in my mind, like echoes of some old movie I once saw but cannot identify. Had those chants come from Tanya in some fever dream, or was I having an auditory hallucination?

The house is cold, but I feel too comfy to retrieve a blanket from the couch. A never-ending block of commercials drones on. My eyes droop, and I become sleepy. As consciousness flees, the chanting rings through my mind, like an alarm bell of the damned.

**

I awake to that groggy feeling one gets while taking a hard nap. My brain is foggy and slow, like someone has poured honey into my ears. Things come into focus.

That damned chanting again...

Which brings my senses to me in a flash, transforming what I thought I heard to the familiar voices of newscasters exchanging chuckling banter after a rare light-hearted story.

"Jeez, how long have I been out?"

I blink away the sleepy haze and look around. Tanya isn't in the living room with me. I grab my phone from the side table where I keep it and look at the display, but it shows me nothing. When I press the button on the side, nothing happens.

"Goddamned thing. Can't be dead."

I try holding the side button to restart it, but the screen remains dark.

"Guess I forgot to charge it after all."

With a stretch, I stand and trudge toward the hallway, figuring I will put my phone on the charger at my bedside.

A mumbling comes from the kitchen.

"I guess you're wondering why I'm not at work," I say, turning into the doorway.

Tanya's mumbling ceases, and she quickly closes a book splayed out on the retro-tiled countertop. She looks up at me like I've caught her in some vile act. Her eyes are wide, and the smile on her face is suspicious, to say the least, which catches me by surprise.

"What's going on in here?" I present a smile of my own to assure her whatever she is doing isn't anything to be ashamed of.

"Nothing. Just looking through an old recipe book and you startled me." She narrows her eyes. "What are you doing home?"

"How long have you been up? You didn't notice the TV on in the living room?"

"I saw you. I left you alone." Her expression levels, eyes slightly cast down. "Figured you weren't feeling well."

"I'm not. I called in."

She nods, and I wonder how the hell she figured something like that? Why didn't she assume I fell back to sleep and wake me up for work?

"You don't look well, Gary."

"Oh?"

Tanya shakes her head. "You're pale. Maybe you should lie down in bed for a while."

"I just fell asleep in the living room. I need to charge my phone."

"Lie down, Gary."

I sigh and walk away. She is in a strange, demanding mood.

"I could use some breakfast," I holler down the hall, making my way to our bedroom.

After putting the phone on the charger—it must be completely dead because the screen doesn't immediately turn on—I decide maybe she's right. Perhaps I need to get off my feet and rest. I feel exhausted, which is unlike me, at least until I get home from work in the evening.

She already made the bed up nice and tidy, so I don't crawl under the covers or anything like that. I just lie on top with my arms folded under the back of my head, eyes closed, and think about those damned sprouts.

My feet begin to tickle and itch. I think nothing of it at first, wiggling them around as best I can to eliminate the minor irritation, but it seems to get worse. Finally, my toes become so itchy they're bothersome. I sit at the edge of the bed and slide my feet out of my slippers, craning my head to examine them.

Nothing out of the ordinary, surely. Maybe just red and inflamed.

I pull my leg up for a closer look.

What I initially think are maggots dangle off my toes. But they aren't...Though I am thankful for this, what I discover is no less ominous and disturbing. The little protrusions are not maggots, but growing eyes of potatoes.

I close my eyes in disbelief. This must be a hallucination. Wiggling them feels natural, but when I open my eyes, I am faced with tiny fingerling potatoes where my toes should be.

So many thoughts enter my mind. Am I suffering from some kind of poisoning which is causing me delusions? Am I trapped in one of those nightmarishly real dreams I cannot wake from?

"Tanya?"

I call for my wife, trying desperately not to sound too dramatic. What I am seeing makes me think I am losing my mind. Surely, she won't brush this off like she does so many of my concerns.

"Just a minute," she says from the kitchen, her voice taking on an almost singsong quality.

Cooking has always been one of her great pleasures. She used to try a new dish every week from one of her cookbooks. I was always her trusty critic, relishing in each new and exotic offering. When she made something truly amazing, we would file it away in the "Dinner Party" file somewhere deep in our minds, as if we would be able to retrieve so many wondrous recipes and choose one to serve to guests at a future date.

We also dreamed of not owning a restaurant, but a food truck, particularly when Tanya used her culinary knowledge and created her own dishes or put a creative spin on a classic.

I glance at my toe again. Nothing has changed. If anything, the little fingerling potatoes look plumper.

"What is it, Gary?" She enters the room, chef's knife in hand.

My breath catches, and my eyes trace the shimmering blade held high. The look on her face—confusion that will quickly dissolve into anger for disrupting her if I don't say something.

"My toes."

She tilts her head and looks at me like I'm a nutjob.

"What are you talking a—" Her eyes slide downward while she speaks. She notices what I'm in distress about. "Holy shit, Gary. What happened to your—"

"You see it too?" I ask.

Tanya nods.

I groan. "Is it what I think it is?"

Tanya kneels at the foot of the bed for a closer examination. Her eyes shine like she is gazing into a chest of gold. She taps the tip of a toe with the knife, and I flinch. Tanya darts her eyes to my face.

"Well, is it?" I ask.

She nods. "Fingerlings, Gary. And they look good. These aren't cheap, you know."

"Aren't cheap?" I squint and tilt my head. "Aren't *cheap*? Why are they growing out of my feet?"

Tanya continues to shake her head, licking her lips as if picturing my toes roasted in the oven around a tri-tip or perhaps a glistening chicken.

"Does it hurt?" She stands, eyes never leaving the strange state of my foot.

I shake my head. "No."

Tanya nods. "I'll call the doctor, see what they say."

"Maybe I need to go to the ER. This…This might be serious."

She shrugs. "Maybe. Let's see what the doctor thinks first, okay?"

With that, Tanya walks out of the bedroom, leaving me confused and fearful of not only the state my toes are in, but the look in Tanya's eyes while she examined them. A hunger was exhibited that gives me a distinct sense of warning.

Moments later, she returns to the bedroom. "The doctor says to keep an eye on things and to call back if it gets worse."

I shake my head. "How much worse can it get, Tanya? Isn't this bad enough?"

"Doctor's orders. Maybe you should get more rest. I'm making a scramble for breakfast." She glances down at my feet. "I used russets, but fingerlings would have done the trick."

With a chuckle, she turns and flees down the hallway to the kitchen. I stare at the doorway in disbelief. How can she joke about a thing like this? Am I overreacting? I don't think so.

The smell of potatoes, onions, and peppers greet me with a one-two punch to my olfactory senses. My stomach grumbles hungrily despite the sense of impending doom I am wallowing in. What does one do when their toes are transforming into little potatoes?

And why is Tanya so nonchalant about it all?

I ponder my peculiar state, trying to convince myself things aren't as dire as they seem. Tanya returns with a steaming plate of breakfast food. I scoot back in bed against the headboard, slipping my toes beneath the sheets to avoid her seeing them, not wanting to bear having her stare while I eat.

After accepting the plate of food and taking a bite, I savor the perfectly seasoned eggs, bacon, and veggies. Tanya could cook this, wrap it in a tortilla with some cheese, and sell them from that food truck of our dreams. She'd make a killing.

"How are the potatoes?" Tanya asks.

I pause my chewing, wondering for a moment if she's asking about the potatoes growing from my foot or the ones I'm eating.

A playful expression on her face further lends to the ominousness of the question.

"Which ones?"

Her smile widens. "The food."

"Great, as always."

"Does it feel...strange? You know, eating potatoes?"

I cringe. "Strange? What do you mean?"

She stands over the bed, watching me like I'm a circus freak.

"You know, considering your toes and all."

How do I answer that?

"It's not funny, Tanya."

"I didn't say it was."

I glare at her, unsure I want to finish my breakfast despite how good the food is. Finally, she looks away, and I can eat in relative peace. I take another forkful of scramble and shovel it into my mouth, enjoying the taste but eager to be finished with the meal. That's when I notice something strange about my finger.

"The fuck is that?" I say, examining it.

"Let me see."

Tanya's voice has an eagerness to it I find disconcerting. She leans in for a close inspection.

"Looks like..." But I don't want to verbalize what I'm thinking.

Never fear. Tanya has no qualms with that.

"Ginger, Gary. Looks like ginger." She uses her nail and digs it into the sandy-colored flesh of my finger, just below a knuckle which eerily resembles a knot on a ginger root.

"Ouch!"

Tanya's mouth makes a surprised "O", like a living blowup doll. "That hurt?"

My face softens. "Well, no, not really...but it was uncalled for."

She tightens her lips in a scowl and shakes her head. Tanya places her finger to her nose and sniffs. Our eyes meet, and I see recognition there.

"Smells like ginger," she says.

My heart lurches. "Oh fuck, what's happening to me?"

"Would you mind if I...?"

*****

Allow Tanya to use a piece of ginger finger for cooking.
Turn to page 118.

Deny her request to use ginger finger for cooking.
Turn to page 20.

I cannot deny the pull this unusual mix of sounds has on me. It's like everything I've ever known all mixed into one. A strange comforting feeling, like sticking close to Mommy in a foreign place. Like coming home after a hard day at work and seeing the smiling faces of my children, smelling the familiar aroma of Deborah's cooking.

I follow my ears and take to the hallway. The sound is coming from the bathroom.

When I turn the corner to peer inside the small space—it has always been contentious for our family of four to share a tiny bathroom with one sink—the interior no longer resembles the bathroom I am so familiar with. I gasp, frozen in place.

The walls are fleshy and raw, undulating with the loud whooshing sound reverberating throughout my entire body. Arturo is nestled into the red, wet nest, trickles of something like afterbirth running down his naked body. Around him are Deborah and the kids, curled into fetal positions.

Arturo says something, but I cannot hear him over the incessant din of this meaty tomb. I am drawn into the room. The womb. I shed my clothes and step inside . . .

***

The correct choice was Ignore the sounds and get some sleep. Turn to page 124.

Staring into the eclipse does not sound like a good idea. The many hollow bodies of *them* crowd around me, pushing into me like strange bubbles of nothing yet frighteningly stifling. I want to scream. They press me against the window, and though I can turn and walk right through them—they aren't even there—I can't shake the feeling they are boring down on me in a way that will drown everything out. Their cold breath and fingers send shivers up my spine and down my arms and legs, appendages like wisps of fine-spun icicles.

I stare out the window at the people enjoying this rare event. The sky darkens, and I am even colder. Under different circumstances, I would be out there with Amy, staring through special glasses, just like the rest of them.

I can't help but wonder if she's sharing this moment with someone else.

Whispers all around assure me I am insane. The voices of the damned, perhaps? Voices of my inner self, escaping like a release of pressure hissing from cracks in my sanity. The voices say so many things, but I cannot focus on them with any sense of coherence.

I bang my fists on the double pane window—one of five installed in the building as replacements. Most of the structure was fashioned with those old double-hung wood-framed atrocities that aren't weatherproof, made out of glass so thin it is amazing they've lasted this long.

No one outside pays mind to my banging. The incessant hissing in my ears from *them* causes me to slam my fists harder. At first, I'm trying to get the attention of the people below, but they either can't hear me or are too intent on the spectacle of the eclipse to give a damn.

I've been showing restraint, as if a glimmer of my consciousness warns me away from possibly shattering the glass. The more *they* crowd in on me, the more the effort at restraint fades. I plow my fists against the glass full force, the pane reverberating with each blow until it gives.

The shatter makes a popping sound when the gas between the two panes is released. The window itself splinters, shards falling into the apartment. I continue to slam my fists, breaking off bits of glass and slashing my palms and wrists. The cuts feel like little bits of nothing, so I continue.

The spirits grab at my bleeding hands, the shapes of their own becoming visible, slathered in blood. I continue to bang at the glass, further damaging my palms on the stubborn edges framing the broken inner pane. The outer won't budge, and no one from below, now beginning to disperse in the aftermath of the eclipse, pays me one iota of attention.

The searing pain strikes me. I cry at the blood running down my arms but continue to pound my fists on the impenetrable glass, now smeared with crimson and casting an eerie orange light into the apartment.

Finally, I give up and retreat to the floor in a pile of bloody glass shards. My wrists are flowing red, and my consciousness leaves. The people of the light swoop in to bask in my arterial flow, fighting over my cut wrists like children on a water hose on the hottest day of summer.

***

Try again. Turn to page 97.

"For Christ's sake, no, you can't cut off a piece of my finger. What, are you crazy or something?"

I try my phone, but it isn't working. Tanya insists the doctor wants me to remain in bed and monitor these unusual growths. It makes no sense to me why we're not going to the ER.

Last year, I had a cough which lingered after I came down with a cold—at least after three negative Covid tests, we called it a cold. She insisted I go to the ER, like I was dying or something. All for a cough. Now, I'm growing produce, and she's calm as placid waters.

"I kind of feel like Thai or Chinese tonight," Tanya says.

"What? How can you think about dinner at a time like this?"

"I dunno. I guess it's the taste of ginger on my lips." She looks at my hand with wanton eyes, and I slip it beneath the covers.

"I need a doctor." I pull my hand out and examine it closer. "It looks like ginger, but it can't be. Is it necrosis?"

"Oh, no, it can't be that. It tastes too good to be rotting flesh."

"Too *good*?"

"It tastes just like ginger." She puts her hand to her chin, clearly in deep thought. "I wonder if I can use a little bit."

"Of my *finger*?"

"Just a tiny bit, that's all."

"Are you crazy?"

"Oh, Gary, I'm just playing with you."

Her voice is too cheery, considering what is happening. She hasn't been like this in years, it seems. I'm reminded of the early days of our marriage, when we were young and eager and so blissfully intertwined. Somewhere along the way, we lost that connection, that joy, that spark. Deep down, it has always bothered me. I yearn for that gleeful innocence, that bit of playful laughter. Now I'm hearing it again, I wonder at what cost.

"I'm going to leave you here to rest. If it gets any worse, call for me, okay?"

I nod. "Okay, dear."

She grins with exaggerated benevolence, and though it would have irritated me only yesterday, it is better than the alternative. Tanya raises her eyebrows as if a thought has occurred to her.

"You know, we're out of garlic, so if you're conjuring produce, help a girl out, would you?"

She leaves and closes the door. I lie in the wake of a callous joke at my expense, as if the changes I am going through are nothing. Something to squawk about to her friends over wine while they shit-talk their husbands.

I place my finger to my nose and take a deep inhale. My senses come alive at the familiar, biting fragrance of fresh ginger. Images swell in my mind, drifting from the deep fathoms of life's memories. It is a smell that will forever remind me of my grandmother's kitchen. The spices and fresh herb aroma always lingered there, as if embedded in the walls and the cabinets. I remember the anticipation of pie on a bright summer afternoon.

Am I dying? It all seems so unreal, to be changing like this. And why isn't Tanya concerned? Why doesn't she help me out to the car and drive me to the emergency room? It makes no sense for my doctor to allow a man with pota-toes and ginger fingers to wait and see how things develop.

They're developing all right. The question is, what's next?

**

When I awake, things are far worse. I *feel* different. There is tightness throughout my body I am unaccustomed to. I look down and don't recognize myself at all.

My potato toes are growing from feet resembling yams. My lower legs and calves are celery stalks connected to my thighs by onions, like ball joints. Whatever the state of my thighs are, I cannot see due to my shorts.

The ginger thumb is now accompanied by four carrot fingers connected to a forearm of summer squash. My elbow is a knobby bulb of garlic. Strangely, my other arm remains normal. I flex my hand and fingers to test this.

"Tanya!" I scream for my wife.

My voice comes out relatively normal, but things have changed. My skin is tight, and my hair seems different. I run my good hand over my head. It feels like grass. With a shudder, I move my hand across my face, tracing the contours of my cheeks and lips. My features seem molded out of wax in some exaggerated manner.

"Tanya!"

Where the hell is she?

After waiting several minutes, yelling for my wife as loudly as I can, I decide to get up. She must have seen me sleeping and gone out, perhaps to get me something from the pharmacy, though I have no idea what would help such an anomalous disfigurement.

I shift forward, attempting to sit up in bed. My body is stuck to the mattress. I pull forward harder. There is a pressure, something tethering me to the bed. Pain erupts in my back, but it is like nothing I have ever experienced before—tendrils of sharp discomfort shooting through my muscle and between my ribs.

My breathing is labored, and I hunch forward. When I look ahead at the mirror on our dresser, I cannot believe my reflection.

Time escapes me. I am in a soundless, weightless void, floating off into the ethers of nothing. In this moment, I cannot, with confidence, say I lost my mind. Those who have gone down that irreversible path to complete mental breakdown and madness might not have any knowledge of such a dire endeavor. I stare at myself, recognizing what has become of me, and I don't know what to make of it.

My hair is a mix of fresh herbs, bright and green. My lips are slivers of red chili peppers. I open my mouth to yellow corn kernels for teeth embedded in corncob gums. These abnormalities are planted in a face still holding onto a human structure, with areas displaying the texture and color of skin, but I am changing quite rapidly. My nose, for instance, is crooked and appears to be contorting into some kind of wrinkled pepper, perhaps a poblano.

My breathing accelerates, and a dizzying wave of nausea comes over me.

"Tanya!"

I call and call for her. She's not there.

I look over my shoulder, struggling to identify the source of the pain coming from my back.

I am rooted to the bed.

Tendrils dangle from my shoulder and spine, the broken ends leaking thick, red sap. The mattress itself has dots of blood and tiny holes indicating where my roots burrowed through before I yanked them free.

I open my mouth to call for Tanya again. She isn't going to respond, so I weep instead. After a few minutes of self-pity, I need to push forward and remove myself from this bed.

When I begin to do so, the pain rages through my body, like electrodes on my nerve endings, and I begin to second-guess myself.

*****

Get up from the bed. Turn to page 38.

Remain in bed and wait for Tanya. Turn to page 24.

The pain radiating from my back is too much for me to take, so I lie down to wait for Tanya's return. There is so much on my mind, and I cannot grab any one thought. How could she leave while I am turning into a living vegetable garden? Where the hell did she go? Is this the work of some strange parasite in my body, like that fungus that turns ants into zombies? How is this even possible?

The roots from my back ease into the mattress. Something is soothing about this sensation, but I know it is wrong. The comforting feeling of being in bed overwhelms me in a way I am not entirely prepared for.

A bed. A bed to sleep. A bed to grow.

A garden bed.

I want to call for Tanya again, but she's not there. The apartment is quiet. I would hear her footfalls, though she can be discreet when she wants. Hopefully, she's getting a doctor, but that is unlikely. Doctors don't make house calls anymore. That is something of a past I know nothing about.

If anything, she will call an ambulance, and the EMTs will have to sever my roots to get me onto a gurney. They will probably have to carry me down the stairs or at least assist me in walking outside to the ambulance.

Is that...? Are those footsteps?

"Tanya?"

A moment later, the door opens. Tanya stands there with a peculiar expression on her face. Not what I would expect from a woman whose husband is mutating rapidly into a bounty of produce. Her eyes almost show compassion. The slight curl of her lips indicates the suppression of a smile. She lets out a breath through her nose, like steam escaping in some old factory—the sure sign she does indeed pity me.

"Have you called for an ambulance?" I ask, as if we discussed that already. I try but cannot keep the exasperation from my tired voice. It's as if my insides are solidifying into organic materials.

She shakes her head. "No, dear."

Tanya approaches the bed. She has something concealed in one hand. Not behind her back, but also purposely out of my line of vision.

"What's that?" I use my good arm to point at her right hand.

"Oh, this?"

She raises a gleaming chef's knife. Normally, I wouldn't think twice about it, assuming she has been busy cooking. Tanya often does that—carries a knife or carrot peeler or whatnot while cooking, if she gets distracted. Under these circumstances, that knife has me worried.

Tanya notices my wary eyes and glances at the knife. "Oh, sorry. I bet a knife like this has a whole new meaning to you now."

Is that wonder in her eyes?

I swallow hard, as if there is a lump in my throat. Or maybe a pearl onion. "What do you mean?"

"Well, you know, with your body going through these changes and all..."

"You didn't call an ambulance?"

"No, Gary. I already told you no. No. No, I didn't."

"I think I need to go to the—"

"Hospital?" Tanya shakes her head. Her lips begin to curl even more, somewhere between a sneer and a devilish grin I don't like one bit. "You don't need a hospital, Gary."

She comes closer, and I am suddenly afraid for my life. This is a Tanya I have never seen before. The lustful look in her eyes is one any man would love to see as a precursor for a sexual encounter, but not like this.

"Look," she says. "I, uh"—a glance at my celery leg—"I'm trying this new recipe, and, um, well, I would hate to see this— you know, *you*—go to waste."

"Go to *waste*?" I scrunch my face, feeling the strangeness of the growths on my skin. "What are you talking about?"

She locks her lips in a way that has me terrified. Why isn't she taking my distress seriously? Why does it appear she wants to—

Tanya reaches out a hand and grabs a rib of celery on my calf, her fingers gently gripping it. A strange sensation runs up my leg like a shiver, so there are nerve endings within the pale green veggie. It is almost a phantom limb sensation, as if it isn't a real part of my body, but some attachment.

She holds the celery tighter. The sensation is not at all unpleasant, just awkward and unsettling. Tanya stares me in the eyes in an almost sexual manner, like a new lover grabbing my penis for the first time. In that moment, I am almost transfixed enough to forget where I am. Then she yanks.

The snap causes my breath to hitch, as if it were a bone, but it is only mildly discomforting.

"There, there. That wasn't so bad, was it?"

Tanya sets the celery aside on the edge of the bed. She poises the knife, and that streak of fear lights me up once again. I shift, trying to back away from her, but my roots are far too tight for me to budge.

"Don't be scared," she says. "I sharpened the knife in the kitchen."

She then places the blade to my stomach, the tip facing upward, and slides it beneath my shirt.

"What are you doing now?" I attempt to keep my voice under control. My breaths come fast and hard—strange in this new body I cannot comprehend.

She lifts the knife, my shirt tight against the blade, and soon the fabric splits. Tanya sets the knife down and uses her hands to tear my shirt wide open.

A scent familiar and yet so very out of place...

An unmistakable fragrance which brings me back to frolicking in my granddaddy's garden. How I used to rub the leaves of his tomato plants—

Where my stomach should be is a cluster of bright red tomatoes in a mess of fragrant leaves.

"Just what I need," she says.

I wince while she yanks the tomatoes from the clutch of the plant embedded in my guts. Though I feel little pain, I am thrown into a world of insane thoughts. A nightmarish vision of my living body being plucked away, one piece at a time, until what is left? How is my mind even functioning? How can this be?

"It's going to be all right." Tanya takes an onion from what once was an elbow. She then reaches for my head, and I am helplessly fixed in place, watching in horror while she grabs a tuft of herbs and rips them in a decidedly more aggressive manner.

Their roots being stripped free is more painful than any of the other bits of me she removed.

With a draw of air and a satisfied exhale of breath from deep within her chest, she says, "That wasn't so bad, was it? Not really what I was expecting at all."

"Expecting?"

Tanya grabs a basket from the dresser, which holds decorative balls that look like twine—something she must have bought at Pier One Imports or T.J.Maxx. She dumps out the contents and replaces them with her bounty. Pieces of me. She says nothing before leaving the room.

I try one final time to move. My roots hold me tight to the bed, so I lie there helpless. In the distance come the sounds of pots and pans and Tanya humming to herself while she prepares something with my vittles.

**

With distinctive *whacks*, Tanya's knife hacks up the very vegetables that grew from my body. I raise my one remaining human limb and marvel at it, wondering why the rest of me has turned into some kind of bizarre plot feeding off me for nutrients, like a normal garden requires soil or hydroponics need water. Why the good arm?

Why didn't I try to stop her from removing my vegetables?

Because I love Tanya.

Despite our differences, despite the stale state our lives have become strangely comfortable in, I love her. Despite the fear and trepidation while she held the knife over me, I cannot imagine putting a hand on her in anger. It isn't in my DNA to harm women, especially my loved ones, no matter how much Tanya can grate on my nerves or, in this case, how eager she is to use me for some culinary delight.

But when I hear the knife chopping through pieces of me, I wonder if maybe I should try harder to survive this. Perhaps I'm allowing her too much leeway in the slow destruction of my bizarre existence.

I hold out my right arm and flex my hand. As a contrast, I lift my left arm and stare numbly at the rigid carrot fingers and bumpy ginger thumb. It appears so delicate. So fragile.

Tanya returns in her apron. This time, she has a meat cleaver in hand—one of those big ones butchers used in the old days. The kind of cleaver with no real place in a tiny apartment—or any average kitchen, for that matter.

I remember when she purchased it, thinking she was going to start buying larger cuts of beef and butchering them down for separate meals—a feat she managed once but found too laborious to continue with any sort of regularity. Eventually, she stashed the massive knife in a drawer.

And here it is, gleaming, menacing, and her yearning to harvest more of my impossible offering of produce.

I open my mouth to say something, to ward her off, but she is determined. That lustful look in her eyes from before has been replaced with something closer to madness with a touch of excitement. She rears the menacing blade back with her right hand, comes in quick, and holds my good arm firmly against the bed.

Before I can react and protect myself, she swings the cleaver hard and swift, making brutal contact with my shoulder. Where I didn't feel pain when she extracted the celery, carrots, and onion, this blow ignites every remaining nerve in my body. My scream is strangled and weird, due to a tongue more like thick lettuce than anything else.

I tense my arm, and Tanya says, "Ease up there, Gary."

Warm blood runs from the laceration. I attempt to free my hand from her restraint.

"One more chop," she says. "I'd hoped I could get it in one, but I guess I'm just not strong enough."

She chuckles to herself, as if there is something funny about what is happening. Then she grits her teeth, eyes blazing, and brings the cleaver down again. This time, she is successful. My arm hits the hardwood floor with a *thump*.

I scream and scream while she walks away. The nub where my last human appendage was feels like it is being seared with a hot poker.

When I try to move, I still cannot. I am rooted to this bed, more food than man. Tired and ready to die.

**

I am in hell. *Truly* in hell. I cannot move, but I can think. And I can smell.

Despite my knowledge of where the mélange of veggies creating such an aroma originated, the scent causes a deep feeling of hunger to rise within me—some final shred of humanity left in a body gone to pasture.

Tanya comes in, this time with a bowl in one hand and an old book in the other. She sets the dish on the bedside table, her eyes never leaving the pages. Her mouth moves while she reads, something I used to find cute that now irritates me. I squint to make out the cover. There are no words, just a circle with a sigil inside I have never seen before.

"What's that you're reading?" I ask, my voice frail. The struggle to speak tells me even my insides are changing. Maybe the end is near?

Hopefully.

Tanya tilts her head, as if wondering whether she should tell me. "It's witchcraft."

I groan, but it sounds strange coming from my new throat.

"It's real, Gary. Me and the ladies have been reading it at our book club meetings. It was a joke at first. Lacey found the books in the basement of a house she's selling. They were all together in an old case. And exactly the number of ladies in our book club."

Tanya laughed and looked away, as if reminiscing on something dear to her heart.

"It was supposed to be a joke, and it *was* a joke on the first night she handed them out. We talked about using the spells to make our husbands do things. It was all a goof until Barbara actually tried one of the recipes. You see, it's not a spellbook, but a cookbook. The recipes *are* the spells. She found a recipe that was supposed to put vitality into a man, and since her husband hasn't been able to get it up in years, with or without the little blue pill, she figured...why not.

"Thing is, it worked. And we could tell." Tanya smirked. "Haven't seen Barbara that happy in a long time. It was like she was floating on air."

It doesn't make sense. I don't believe in magic. But I also don't believe in men turning to vegetables.

"What did you do to me?"

She stares down at me and smiles. Then she reads passages from the book, intoned like some chanting monk, and it is then that I put some of the pieces together. The chanting I swore I heard from the bedroom...She worked on this for days, if not weeks.

Tanya places the book on the edge of the bed, grabs the bowl, and kneels beside me. She guides a spoonful of soup to my mouth. I don't want it but find I have little choice.

What have I got to lose? I have allowed her to pluck from my sprouted body and claim the final morsel of my flesh. This is the end, and though I am having a hard time accepting she did this to me on purpose, I don't have any fight left.

I taste the soup. Despite my reservations, my sadness and frustration, it *is* good. Tanya is a wonderful cook.

She smiles while I eat and tells me what horrors I have accepted upon this meal of fate.

"I love to cook, as you know, and so I thought of how wonderful it would be to have a garden right here inside the apartment. Fresh vegetables for any dish I desire. And now that I have said the words and you have drunk of your own bone broth, the spell is complete. You, Gary, are my garden."

I have no words.

"That's the broth. Gary's Bone Broth." That smile. So menacing. "Now I want to make a soup. A vegetable soup."

The smile fades, replaced by determination and cunning. She grabs two of my carrot fingers and snaps them off without the gentle care she took previously. Tanya yanks two ribs of celery, another onion, a couple of garlic cloves, and some herbs from my head. I feel each removal. Not so much the pain of it, just a sensation, like being slowly plucked away by carrion.

She grabs my shorts and pulls them down, her eyes gleaming. That sick smile spreads across her face yet again.

"You know, I always thought those text emojis of the eggplant were kind of misleading." Tanya nods. "This is more what I expect, and I sure do love mushrooms in my vegetable soup."

Mushrooms grow where my manhood once was. She grabs them with no sense of delicacy or concern, pulling them out by the roots.

I lie here in this bed I'm rooted to and regenerate. She plucks away at me, and I wonder if this will ever end.

Try Not to Die in This Damned House II

The interesting thing about the model of Greenwood Planes that rests atop a huge table in Markus's attic is that his house, nestled atop a hill overlooking the town, was not included. His great-grandfather built the house many years ago. Markus wasn't certain, but assumed there was nothing in the valley at that time. He'd been told his great-grandfather built the first dwellings in Greenwood Planes, though Markus wondered if the man discovered something on that property which allowed him to create the town right there in that attic.

During his downtime between tormenting apartments and the locals, Markus often examined the structure his Greenwood Planes model rested upon. The top was covered with model buildings and trees and even dirt. But underneath, by using a flashlight, Markus could better see the pattern of the marble slab or granite—or whatever material it was made of.

It looked nothing like anything he'd ever seen before. Nothing like the tabletops on countless home improvement shows he'd watched on TV, like *This Old House* or *Flip This House*. Being he fancied himself a homebuilder, he was constantly fascinated with such shows.

Not that Markus built the houses from actual lumber and materials found in the Home Depot forty minutes away, in the nearest big city. He made the structures of modeling materials in his attic, just like his grandfather did before him.

The strange granite slab rested on an elaborate set of legs built of wood taken from the yard. This he knew only because the pieces had knots and bark where it wasn't planed smooth for construction purposes. The pieces of wood were all connected through intricate tongue and groove, proving his great-grandfather knew something about carpentry. The structure was tight and sturdy. Markus often marveled at it, almost sad such craftsmanship had not been handed down through the generations to him.

He blamed his father for that. The man was a drunk. He'd disregarded the model of Greenwood Planes for who knows how long before Markus was old enough to wander into the attic and discover it. It should have been a family tradition, handed down from generation to generation, like something coveted and special, a mystical heirloom.

An alarm rang from an old clock radio, the high-pitched screeching almost like the violins during the shower scene in *Psycho*. Markus sighed and pressed the button to silence it.

It was feeding time.

Markus scanned the attic for the item he would place in the next apartment window. His eyes fell upon a mop leaning against the wall. It had been quite a while since he mopped the attic floor. He'd never been much of a cleaner, spending his entire life as a bachelor.

Well, a bachelor of sorts. There *was* another mouth to feed these days, but that didn't make him feel any less a man alone in his house. A man who took pleasure in watching people suffer.

He clipped a strand of fiber from the mop head and pushed it through the window of the little fourplex apartment. Markus considered taking a gander through the telescope but knew better. These things took time. His manipulations were never immediate.

And besides, it was feeding time.

No Job is Too Dirty

When we enter the old lady's house, the last thing we expect to find is her husband's body butchered in the fucking living room. She is so sweet when she answers the door. Hers is a smile promising cookies and candy, hot cocoa and a slice of pie—not the brutal slaying of the man she grew old with!

I'll back up a minute. My name is Garvey Edwards, and I run No Job Is Too Dirty Cleaning Services, which is to say I operate a very small business with my partner and protégé, Dan Wompler. I call him Danny Boy sometimes because it irritates him, and you know how that is. When you find out what gets under your coworker's skin, you use that shit like ammunition.

Danny Boy has a lot to learn. He's still green, but he's getting the hang of things. Danny was one of those troubled kids no one would give a break to. In and out of juvie. Broken home. You know the story. Has a bit of a reputation here in Greenwood Planes. Whereas everyone else sees a bad apple, I recognize someone who can be molded into a productive member of society.

Poor bastard doesn't know what to think when he sees the blood. Neither do I, for that matter. We've cleaned crime scenes, yes, but the body is always long gone. My company specializes in that kind of stuff, along with bad rental move-outs requiring the deepest of cleanings. Can't be squeamish in this business. But this is something so out of our realm, we just stand here dumbfounded.

"So, what do you think, boys?" the old woman says.

I glance at her and kind of shake my head, still at a loss for words. She's looking at me with that welcoming grin, as if there's nothing at all unusual about the three of us all but wading in the small pool of her husband's blood.

She tells us to call her Jan. Kind of an old-school name. The woman is old enough to be my grandmother, but there's something menacing about her. Maybe the dead guy on the floor,

I don't know. Something behind her smile has me on edge. Dan's shaking in his boots. He wants out, but he's smart enough to leave the first move to me.

"Um..." I try to open up a conversation, but I'm just not sure what the fuck to say to her. "So, what, uh...What happened here?"

Her smile widens, hiding an evil sneer barely rearing its ugly head. Right then and there, I can tell she is two-faced. Her poor husband has seen that other side. Well, *did.*

"Well, you see," she begins, "Thomas was in the living room watching his cooking shows—he fancies himself a chef, but he hardly knows his way around a kitchen. I told him and I told him I had to get the table ready for Bunco tonight. That is to say, I needed his help with the leaf to lengthen the table. My Bunco group is quite large, and this is my week to host."

She shakes her head with a sigh of grief and stares at the remains of Thomas.

"He knows when it's my week. If he's such a good chef after watching all those damned cooking programs, why doesn't he get off his ass and prepare something for me and the ladies?" The old woman shakes her head even more. "Nope. Just sits there like a fat slug. Can't even get him up to help with putting the leaf in the table."

There is no mistake. She murdered him. But hearing about it is sick. Leave the old slug, but don't kill the poor bastard. I am about to say something—not sure what, all things considered, but something!—when she continues her tirade.

"He's been lazy all his life, I suppose. Sure, he worked and brought home the bacon, but he was worthless around the house. I raised the kids...Did the cooking, cleaning, washing...everything. He sat there watching his programs. Back then it was *M*A*S*H* and college football. Now he watches that food channel all day." A deep sigh. "Never have seen him cook a damn thing in his life."

"You know what?" I say. She locks eyes with me in a way that freezes me up, very much like I am about to be scolded, which causes me to feel like a complete fool. "I don't think this is the job for us." Now I shake my head. "We're pretty booked up, ma'am. I didn't realize it was going to be this extensive."

"But your ad says no job's too dirty?"

"Yes, ma'am, but you see, we've been very busy lately and—"

"And *nothing*." She takes a step toward me.

Dan might have flinched, but who knows.

"I hired you for this job. You said, on the phone, that it would be no problem."

"On the phone, you said you needed the living room cleaned ahead of your bingo game."

"It's *Bunco,* not bingo. And the ladies will be here in a matter of hours." Her eyes become fierce orbs which seem to glow. "I need to have this place cleaned before they get here." She put her hands out, shaking her head. "I just can't have them seeing this...this...this *mess*."

"I'm sorry, ma'am, but we're not the right guys for this job. Come on, Dan. Let's call it a day."

"Like hell you're not!"

Her voice rings out like a shotgun blast echoing off the walls of the room. We both turn for the door and stop, exchanging a knowing glance.

*****

Turn around and try to communicate with her.
Turn to page 43.

Ignore her and try opening the front door.
Turn to page 121.

I grit my teeth and pull forward against the hold these insufferable roots have on me. The pressure on my back is immense and uncomfortable, but I cannot imagine being tied to the bed like this, especially alone in the house. Each root breaks, the disconnection causing snaking jolts of pain to course through my flesh, like being stabbed with a knife.

One after the other, I pull myself free, screaming against the agony—both my natural reaction and a way to alert Tanya, if she is still somewhere in the apartment. At this point, I am happy to notify *anyone* of my state. I am in dire need of an ambulance.

Fairly certain the roots have all been severed, I sit at the edge of the bed for a moment. Will more snake from my body and into the mattress before I can gain my bearings and stand?

After several deep breaths, I do just that.

My first few steps are as unsteady as a drunk at the end of a long night of consumption. I take several lumbering advances and brace myself with the dresser, close enough to give my face a better inspection than I could from my position in the bed.

My chili pepper lips part, and I am horrified at the bright yellow of my corn teeth. Scallions grow from my bumpy cucumber chin like a thick beard. Eyebrows of some kind of micro green or chia hover over a pair of despondent eyeballs, which remain as human as they were before my body went to seed. My ears resemble little cauliflowers—an almost comical representation of a classic boxing injury, only I can't muster even the slightest laughter in this moment of total despair.

I move unsteadily on feet of potato, struggling at first to grip the door handle with my carrot and ginger fingers before realizing I still have a normal arm, for some reason. It appears to be my only good appendage. I grip the door with said hand. It feels right.

The familiar hallway is lined with family photos. I make to call for Tanya again, but something stops me. A sound. That strange chanting I heard in the morning. It is coming from the other bedroom. That is our catchall room, officially labeled a spare bedroom but in no shape for company.

"Tanya?"

The chanting continues in a language I cannot understand. There's something Latin about the words but with no distinct cultural dialect I can pinpoint. And why is Tanya in the spare bedroom while I'm suffering in bed? She has often become insufferable with old age, and we have certainly grown apart, but I assumed we would always be there for one another in our times of need, those base feelings resurfacing when push comes to shove.

Anger erupts, causing my weird body to feel even stranger. I can't help but wonder what my brain looks like. Is it a cabbage or, better yet, an extension of the cauliflower sprouting from my ears? And what about my organs? I have to assume my heart has molded into a beet.

With a shake of my head, I run my good hand over my face, appalled at the bizarre texture of vegetables, like a living cornucopia. I cry but no tears come. Maybe it's thick sap or the morning dew running down my cheeks to feed my tortured body.

"Tanya!" I raise my voice, grip the door handle, and open it.

The chanting ceases, and I am faced with something just as incomprehensible as the tiny roots holding my celery legs to my onion-jointed knees. The floor in the room has been cleared. Boxes and detritus are pushed against the walls and piled atop the little twin bed in the corner. On the floor is a pentagram with black candles alight.

Tanya stands on the other side, as bare as the day she was born. Her saggy breasts dangle like fruit, though still resembling an older woman's body. She looks at me with fierce intensity, not so much because I interrupted her ritual, but as if she has been waiting for me.

"What is this?" My voice is strange and foreign. Perhaps my throat has turned into a rutabaga.

"Just look at you, Gary," she says, marveling at my horrid state.

"What's happening to me?"

I am appalled at the bizarre scene before me and yet am in such a terrible way that base emotion takes over. All I want is for Tanya to hold me, help me, love me. I hold out my arms, both the good one and the amalgamation of produce. She does the same, with a smile and eyes like glassy balls of fire.

I step forward, unconcerned about the candles and the pentagram painted onto the hardwood. Candles can't do anything to me anyhow. My body is too fresh, the water content of my fruiting appendages too rich for mere candle fire to harm.

"Come here, honey," she says.

And for a moment, I feel as if she will console me and things will be, as absurd as it sounds, all right.

I step forward, through the circle around the star. First one potato foot and then the next. Only once I'm inside the circle, I cannot move. Tanya's smile widens.

"I'm so glad you came on your own volition," she says. "That makes things so much easier. And it pleases my master."

Panic rises. "What...What's going on? I can't move. I *can't move!*"

"*Shhhhhh*. Calm down," she coos. "It's okay."

"It's *not* okay. What the hell is going on? Why can't I move?"

"This is the way he wants it. This is the way *I* want it."

"Want what?"

"You."

"Me?"

Tanya nods. Her body shimmers in the glow of candles. "The sacrifice."

Dark lines accentuated by the saggy nature of her flesh create a frightening visage hardly resembling the woman I love, almost as if it is someone else. But she has the same birthmark on her lower stomach, just above her pubis, and the scars running the length of her thighs from a horrible car wreck many years ago—distinguishable markings on the woman I know intimately, the woman who has been practicing black magic behind my back.

It takes a moment for the word to sink in. "Sacrifice?"

Tanya nods. "I want for nothing, Gary, and yet I find I am always wanting more. I don't want to live in this shitty little apartment any longer. I don't want to live on a budget because of your poor decisions. I told you, you should have gotten a better job with benefits, but no. You had to do things your way. We shouldn't struggle at our age, Gary."

She glares at me with flames reflected in her sparkling eyes.

"I met some people, Gary. People you don't know. Other ladies of a certain age who have become tired of their boring old lives. We've been dabbling. Oh, is it witchcraft? Satanism?" Tanya shakes her head. "I don't think any of us really know. It started as a game, just for fun, but the thing is, Gary, it works."

I stare at my wife while she speaks incomprehensible rubbish, and I cannot move a muscle. Not that much of me is muscle anymore. I can't move so much as a carrot, paralyzed, helpless to her maddening words.

"One of my new friends, Barbara, was the first to try it out. A recipe from a strange cookbook Lacy found in an old house she was showing. Lacy's a real estate agent, Gary. Thing about these recipes is that they are not all for food. And even those invoke something different, something occult. We thought it would be a laugh, and so we practiced the spells that accompany some of the recipes. Barbara took it a step further and used a recipe on her husband. A pie that made him virile."

She pauses as if wanting me to say something.

"And guess what? The following night, it was as if his impotence was a thing of the past."

"I don't suffer from impotence," I say.

"No, you don't. That's not what this is all about. That's what Barbara wanted out of her husband. I just want to live without a worry in the world, and you've been the source of my misery.

Don't you see? You always told me I wouldn't have to work, that I could take care of the home and you would be the breadwinner, but that really hasn't worked out for me, and I'm getting just a little bit tired of living on a goddamned budget every goddamned week. This is *not* what I signed up for."

"What are you going to do?" My words come out weak and shaky. I dart my eyes downward.

All of my body has transformed. There is no longer anything human left of me. Just my thoughts and a voice not only growing weaker by the second, but restricted, probably by tonsils turning into Brussels sprouts or some such organic matter.

Tanya comes close. I haven't seen her like this since we were first dating. Back then, it was a look of hungry lust, when our desire was hot and we pined for one another like animals in heat. Now, I have no idea what the carnal look in her eyes means.

"I am going to consume you," Tanya says. "Every last bit of you. Starting with the greens on your head, into the broccoli brain—or will it be cauliflower?—right down to the potatoes at your feet. You have brought me a world of wanting. Once I consume you, I will want for nothing. I will be a free woman."

I try to speak, but my vocal cords are completely restricted now. Tanya leans in and grabs a handful of the herbs and sprouts from my head. She puts them into her mouth and chews like a cow on cud, eyes never leaving mine. Tanya plucks a bit of cauliflower from where my right ear used to be.

My vision slowly fades, turning red. My eyeballs transform to what I can only imagine are cherry tomatoes.

I can now see nothing. But I feel Tanya picking pieces of me, one at a time.

Soon enough, I feel nothing at all.

***

The correct choice was Remain in bed and wait for Tanya.
Turn to page 24.

We stop, and I glance over at Dan, who is looking at me. He's a tough hombre, but there's something in his eyes I don't like.

Being rough on the streets is one thing. I've spent hours talking to Danny Boy and know what type of man he is. An intimidator. A gritty guy who pushes out his chest and has probably only had to fight a few times. He managed to create a reputation by merely *acting* like he is some hot shit. I know his type. Thing is, even the most hardened guy will be terrified in the presence of a mutilated body, even if the perpetrator *is* an old woman.

I turn to face Jan. Dan does the same. I look into her eyes with what I hope is something close to empathy, though I have little of that in stock. That's when it occurs to me: Perhaps there is some deeper reason for her to have committed this heinous act.

They say a crime of passion is one of many stab wounds or gunshots. The fella on the floor has been chopped to ribbons. His face could be scooped up and sold as minced meat at a butcher's counter. It's only now I notice the cleaver sticking out of the mess she made of his gut. What she did might have been a long time in coming.

"What did he do to you?" I ask, voice low and even, hoping this will be a good way to connect with this crazy old bitch.

She scrunches her face, like I made an off-color comment. "Do to me? What do you mean?"

I nod toward the body. "To do something like that to him, I figure he must have done something pretty bad. Maybe over many years. Did he hurt you?"

Somehow, her face furrows even more. "Oh, get off it, Dr. Phil. The lazy son of a bitch wouldn't move a muscle to help, and I've got Bunco tonight. A lot goes into preparing for Bunco. He has to clear out of here on Bunco night. Watch TV in the bedroom. Is that asking too much?"

I shake my head. But I want to ask, *Is that a reason to murder him?* Yet I know better. This woman is a couple cans short of a six-pack.

Jan continues. "I have cleaning, cooking, setting up the table..." She levels her eyes on mine. "Do you know he wouldn't help me with the leaf in the table?"

I just stare at her and shake my head, which might be misconstrued as an understanding. God forbid he didn't help her with that fucking leaf. Off with his head! And she tried. His neck is a bloody mess that looks like blackberry cobbler.

Dan remains silent. I can't blame him. But he's not the tough guy everyone thinks he is, that's for sure. Is there a spot of saturation on his pants? There's not, but it wouldn't have shocked me had the kid pissed himself.

"Time's a wastin'," Jan says. She glances at the cleaning supplies we brought in. "You have your stuff ready to go, so get to it." She looks at her watch—who the hell still wears a watch! "Only three hours before the ladies start arriving, and you can count on that Deborah to be early. Nosey as all get out."

"We can't do this," I say.

"You what?" She reaches for the cleaver handle and rips it from her husband's corpse. It makes a slick squelching noise when it slides free of his minced guts. Ropes of coagulating blood drip from the blade.

"We'll do it," Dan blurts out.

I crane my head and squint my eyes in confusion. He's so terrified he's shaking. I'm scared too, but come on. It's an old lady. We can both take her down if we have to.

That cleaver is quite menacing. She has a good grip on it. Steady hands. We had a chance against her—if it came to that— until she grabbed the fucking cleaver. If the blade is honed, it will cut right through bone, no problem. Even if she lacks the strength to do that, it will do some serious damage. She has the advantage, that's for sure.

Dan grabs a mop, which is ridiculous. If we *were* going to clean this crime scene, mopping would be one of the *last* things we do. He's just nervous and jittery, and I can't blame him. When he signed up to clean filthy hoarder houses and crime scenes, this is not what he expected.

I glance down at our supplies, then look back to Jan and her cleaver. "You have heavy-duty garbage bags? I, uh, wasn't expecting…this. I didn't bring any in with me." I did. They are at the bottom of my five-gallon bucket. "I'll go out and get a few bags if I need to."

"You'll go out and do nothing. I have bags." She darts her eyes to Dan at my left, and her face scrunches up. "What's he doing?"

I look over my left shoulder. Dan is pushing a mop through the blood. The gray mop head is now saturated and doing nothing but smearing crimson around the floor. The kid has fucking lost it.

I look back at Jan with piteous eyes. "What do you expect? He snapped."

"Snapped? What the hell for? This is what you two do for a living."

"Are you kidding? We don't do this."

"'No job's too dirty.' That's what your advert says. What are you, a liar?"

I think of several nasty things to say to this crazy woman, but I refrain. There is something about her which reminds me of my own grandmother, though I can't imagine Grandma losing her shit and killing my grandfather.

"The bags?" I ask with a sigh.

"Follow me."

She turns, and I feel a jolt of excitement. This is the moment I have been waiting for. I hesitate. How absurd would I be to tackle an old woman to the ground? In that moment of hesitation, she turns on me with the cleaver raised.

"And don't try anything funny." The look in her eyes is terrifying. The speed at which she spins around shocks me. "I'm watching you. I might be an old woman, but I'm not feeble. I was a track runner and a dancer all my life, and I stay limber. That's a key to longevity, you know. Staying limber. I do puzzles too. Keeps the brain thinking. Thomas sat his ass in front of that TV all the damn time. Turned his brain into mush, you ask me."

I look back at Dan, then enter the kitchen through a doorway. It also leads to a hall where the bedrooms and bathroom are located. Dan swirls a bloody mess, like a forlorn janitor with nothing left in his mind.

The kitchen is clean. The counters are lined with prep for whatever snacks she plans to make for Bunco tonight. Jan crouches and opens the cabinet beneath the sink. She rifles through the contents with one hand, keeping a tight grip on the cleaver with the other.

"Ah, here we go." Jan rises, clutching several thick, black trash liners. "Here we are." Her voice rings out like a loving grandmother who just finished baking a cherry pie.

"What are you making?" I ask.

"Excuse me?"

"For Bunco?"

"Oh!" Her inflection changes on a dime. She smiles. "Well, I'm making a spinach and artichoke dip, of course. Everyone raves about it." She narrows her eyes. "Unless, of course, Suzan brings that nitwit husband of hers if we have a cancellation. He doesn't like anything. I've got a cheese tray, but Genevieve is lactose intolerant, not that anyone really believes her." Jan lowers her voice. "If you ask me, I think she purges and looks for any excuse not to eat. And I made a delightful crumb cake for when we have coffee later. I don't know one person who can resist my crumb cake. It's world famous, you know."

"That sounds wonderful." I try to keep a sense of cheer in my voice, but it's fake.

Jan tilts her head, eyes narrowing yet again. "You're not trying to get some food out of me, are you? Don't even think about it, cleaner boy. The food is strictly for Bunco. My son used to try and eat everything before the Bunco crew got here, and it drove me nuts." She shakes her head. "That ungrateful son of a bitch! One time, he stuck his fingers in the icing on a cake I'd baked. I hadn't even noticed until I pulled it out to serve. Do you know how embarrassing that was?"

I shake my head. "I wasn't indicating that I wanted food."

"All you're here for is to get rid of Thomas's body. So, get to it!" She thrusts the bags out, and I grab them too eagerly.

I want nothing to do with this grisly affair, and yet I'm not entirely sure how to get away without causing a scene.

When we get back into the living room, Dan is pushing blood around with the mop like that guy in Nirvana's "Smells Like Teen Spirit" video. I open my mouth to say something and then think better of it. What *can* I say? He's fucking lost it already. Poor fool.

"So, just how are we supposed to get him out of here without it looking like we're doing exactly what we're doing?" I ask.

"Excuse me?" Jan says. "I don't follow."

"Well, we wrap Thomas here up in bags, and then what? You expect us to waltz right out of here and through the lobby like we're not carrying out a stiff?"

"You're not carrying him out the front door, my dear."

"Then what do you have in mind?"

"The garbage shoot."

"The…?"

Jan nods. "What do you think I am? Stupid? Of course we can't carry him out the front."

"How do you propose we use the garbage shoot?"

Jan shakes her head. "You cut him up."

She tilts her neck, eyes and lips drawn to tight slits, gears working while she contemplates things. I hope she's coming to her senses, but how can she? This psycho granny killed her husband. No matter what she does, she's either ending up in prison or doing her best to cover up this crime, which now involves both myself and Danny Boy.

"Better yet," Jan says, "I'll cut him up myself. I don't need you and your helper—by the way, what the hell is wrong with him? He kind of slow or something?"

I pivot my head. Danny Boy swirls gore in circles with a mop so saturated, the blood is beginning to coagulate into dark chunks.

"He's freaked out, ma'am."

"For Christ's sake. Don't be such a pussy."

She disappears into the kitchen. It's my chance to make a move.

"Danny," I whisper, but he continues his work like a fucking lunatic. "Danny!"

He's gone. I've seen this sort of thing in the movies but didn't know it happened in real life. Danny is ready for the white padded room and a straightjacket. This one flew into the cuckoo's nest and bedded down nice and tight.

Not wanting to leave Danny in a situation like this but not knowing what else to do, I go for the front doorknob and twist, but it won't budge. Is it one of those handles which locks from both the inside and out? I look at it closely.

It's not. There's no reason it should be stuck like this. I try it again, and it won't even turn.

"The fuck?" I mutter beneath my breath.

"And just what the hell are you doing?" Jan reenters the room, startling me.

"I left some cleaners in the car. We're going to need the extra strength stuff for dealing with all this blood."

"The hell you did. Get away from that door. I was a world champion track runner once upon a time. And I keep fit and in shape. Don't doubt my age, boy. I'll dash across this room and have this cleaver buried deep in the back of your head before you can so much as consider your defense."

In one hand, she holds the cleaver, a large, wooden cutting board in the other. It is thick and looks heavy, the surface discolored from years of use. Have any other humans have been butchered on it?

"Can't be putting gouges in the floor." She slides the cutting board beneath her husband's outstretched arm.

Danny continues to swirl chunky stuff into a macabre rendition of Van Gogh's *Starry Night*. Jan raises the cleaver and brings it down with not so much as a pause of consideration. The force is enough to break the bone, but it takes one more whack to sever the forearm.

With each hammer of the cleaver, I cringe and clench my teeth. Danny Boy finally ceases his nervous swirling, opting to clutch his mop handle and cower against the wall. If we get out of this, he'll never be the same.

I need to get that mop. The handle will give me enough length to attack and defend myself from that massive cleaver.

A couple more sharp whacks and the old man's upper arm is severed. The blood has long ceased pumping from the heart but leaks from the stump at his torso. It's thick and dark, like ripe cherries or syrup from a spilled bottle.

I want to make my move, but Jan looks over her shoulder at me constantly. She's agile for her age. There are pictures on the wall of a younger Jan running track, and gold medals shine in a frame above the fireplace across the room. Was she an Olympian? How did she get to be so vicious?

Another several wet hacks and his leg is severed. The sound sticks in my brain on repeat, like nothing I've ever heard before. A dull *thump*, like axing a log, matched with something gelatinous and a sucking sound when she pulls the embedded blade from the meat. Maybe it's so gross because it's a man and not a side of beef, but I really don't know.

I look at Danny, hoping for eye contact. If only I can get him out of his mad daze, we can take her. There's no doubt about it.

But one wrong move and that cleaver is going to end me. I have no doubt about that either.

"What the hell are you waiting for?" Jan asks. "Get a bag and start wrapping this up. Bunco starts in a few hours, and I still have a load of preparations. Should be you down here, doing this dirty work, but I just don't think I can trust you with a knife."

"I can cut him up," I say without thinking. I don't want to, but I want that cleaver.

"Just bag him. I got this."

I hesitate.

"*Now!*"

Before I know it, I'm on the ground with a black trash liner, stashing limbs into it and then rolling everything into a tight bundle. Jan slides the heavy cutting board beneath each limb before swinging the cleaver, like she'd been a butcher all her life and not a track star.

Danny remains against the wall, clutching his mop like that nerdy kid who turns into the Toxic Avenger. He can make a move, but he's too far gone. I pity him as much as I'm angered he's so weak, considering what a tough guy he convinced the entire town of Greenwood Planes he is.

I collect the left leg into two bundles, wrapping them in the duct tape Jan provided. There's blood all over my hands, and I'm disgusted I didn't use gloves. The fear got to me. I haven't been thinking as much as doing. With each bundle of Thomas's body parts, I can't help but anticipate the cleaver coming for me. There's no way this madwoman is letting us out of here, right?

Finally, she dismembers the entire body, leaving only his head. One of his eyes sticks out of the mess she made of him and stares up at the ceiling. Part of his mouth was caught in a scream, teeth missing, probably lodged in his throat or maybe jettisoned beneath the couch during whatever struggle happened when Jan lost her shit and attacked him.

"Thomas, you old son of a bitch." Jan raises the bloody cleaver. "You always were a lazy, good-for-nothing piece of shit.

All the work I put into keeping fit and working hard at winning and all you did was sit on the couch like a loser. I really don't know what I ever saw in you or why I spent so much time...Till death do we part, asshole."

She swings the cleaver down in a fierce thrust, gripping it with both her hands. It slices through his neck with ease, then clinks on his spine, making a cracking noise but not dislodging his head from the torso. Chunks of gore cast off his jellied face and onto the walls and furniture.

Jan makes a low growling noise, rears the cleaver, and brings it down with as much ferocity as the first time. The blade slams into the cutting block, lodging there. The head launches away from the body, taking rest at Danny's feet.

Danny loosens his grip, and the mop falls to the floor. His eyes widen, and his mouth drops. He gently kicks the head away from him before going into hysterics. Danny screams like a child, tears running down his face.

I've never seen anything like it. A complete breakdown. He's a kid having a tantrum.

"Shut up!" Jan yells. "Stop it!"

She pulls the cleaver back, and I know what she's going to do.

*****

Intervene in an attempt to stop her attack on Danny Boy.
Turn to page 6.

Grab the mop and attack Jan. Turn to page 115.

Turn away so as not to see her attack on Danny Boy.
Turn to page 60.

I've threatened to call Amy so many times it's sick, finger hovering over the send button on my phone. Or even a text message with a pathetic apology.

I suck in an acrid drag from a butt burned all the way down to the filter, grimace, and connect the line.

Amy answers with a breathless sigh. "What do you want?"

What do you want? What kind of way is that to answer the phone?

"I'm so glad you answered," I say, feeling like a tool and wanting to punch myself in the face.

"Look, it's over between us. It's nothing personal, really. We just don't mesh."

"But I thought we did—"

"We don't. I'm telling you, we don't."

"But why?"

Another sigh. She regrets answering the phone. I can tell.

"Someday, you'll meet the right girl. It's just not me."

"But you *are* the right girl. I know you are."

I sound fucking pathetic, but I cannot seem to stop myself.

"It's over between us, and this is partly why. Can't you just take 'no' for an answer?" Another one of her sighs, like a dagger in my ear. "You need to seek help from a professional."

"What's that supposed to mean?"

"Exactly what I said. Seek help. You're a good guy, but sometimes, you are hard to be around. Maybe you have some things you need to work through. Consider therapy. It really helps."

"Therapy?"

"Okay, I'm done here—"

"Wait, wait, sorry. You're right, okay. You're right. Maybe I *should* get therapy."

"Have a great life."

"I have some therapy right now."

A pause. "What?"

"I'm holding some therapy in my hand."

"What are you talking about?"

"I'm going to drag this therapy right across my neck."

"Wait, what?"

I slice the knife across my throat. The blade bites into my soft flesh effortlessly. My scream is involuntary, but I manage to somewhat control it.

"Take that!" I gurgle, blood filling my throat.

Amy's screams are the last thing I hear as I collapse onto the floor.

***

The correct choice was to Leave Amy in the past.
Turn to page 83.

My children are softly crying, and though I am not in control of Arturo's motions, I do everything I can to will him to the door on the left. More than anything, I want to see my kids again, but not like this. There is no way to change the past, and yet there's this feeling within my consciousness, as if I can avoid the horrors perpetrated on my children by avoiding their room entirely.

Hand on the door to our master bedroom, I turn the handle slowly. I cannot hear Deborah, but I know she's in there. Probably cornered in fear and doing everything she can to keep quiet. She worries about Hope and Gabriel—I know that for a fact. But also, she's hurt. The trail of red drops on the hardwood lead to the room. The stickiness coats my hands when I open the door.

Inside, everything is dark.

She should have attacked me right when I opened the door. That would have been her best chance at subduing me. Well, Arturo. There's no way she thinks it is me, right?

"Little Debbie?" My voice is not my own. It belongs to Arturo. There's no way she mistook him for me. I never once called my wife "Little Debbie."

"Come and give me your cupcake, Little Debbie."

I flick the light on. The room is empty, but a line of blood droplets guide me to the closet. I chuckle, almost choked by the phlegm in my throat from years of smoking. That is a nasty habit Arturo picked up when we were teenagers—another idiosyncratic difference between us. I hate tobacco. Always have.

"I know you're in there," I say. "I remember when my brother met you. I remember when he introduced you to the family. Flaunting you like some prize. Little Debbie. I wanted to break you open and taste your cream right from day one." I shake my head. "But no. Despite us looking the same, my brother always got the girl. Always got the good job. Always got the bulk of love from our mother and respect from our father. By the time they came to me, there was nothing left. Try living with that all your life, cupcake."

The house is quiet. The door remains open, and yet I cannot hear Gabriel and Hope. Nothing but the creaking floorboards beneath my feet.

"You can come out now," I say. "No use hiding when I know you're in here."

Still no movement.

I slip my fingers into the handle of the sliding closet door and open it in one quick motion. Deborah is on the other side, crouched amongst clothes hanging from a dowel. She leaps forth with a war cry and my hunting knife. Inside, I'm smiling, happy she is defending herself. But I know the outcome.

I jerk out of the way of the blade and her. She overcompensates, thrusting the weapon with all her might. Her body launches onto the hardwood, the knife slamming into the floor at least an inch.

My hand reaches out and grabs a tuft of her hair, yanking violently. Her scream is more of a yelp. I pull so hard a clump of hair comes out, the roots bloody from the crude extraction.

With a smile I say, "I guess it's not cream inside this Little Debbie. More like cherry filling."

She wastes no time feeling sorry for herself or wallowing in the pain inflicted upon her. Deborah grabs my leg and pulls, causing me to lose balance and tumble to the floor. When I go down, I use my other foot to kick her in the face.

It isn't the hardest, but enough to knock her off-balance again. Only for a moment. She grits her bloody teeth and fights back. Deborah is wiry and agile, moving like a ferocious animal.

After blocking her swinging arms and legs, I grab her by the throat with one beefy hand. The grip is so perfect, as if her throat was made to be squeezed. This doesn't stop her from squirming, but slows things down a bit. I thrust her body backward, lifting myself from the floor, and pin her to the wall, slamming the back of her head.

"Goddamn! Do you have that kind of enthusiasm in the bed?"

Deborah struggles, but my hand around her throat is tight. The pressure on her larynx causes her to choke and cough. Soon enough, she weakens, and her body wilts beneath the domineering hold.

I let go. Her hands reach for her throat and rub her neck. Terrified eyes watch me while I unzip my pants. A thick rope of spit hangs from my mouth, and I feel like the monster I am. Not *my* consciousness, but the body I inhabit.

"Don't make this hard," I say, then laugh. "Well, I guess it's gonna *get* hard...But don't fight me, Little Debbie, or you're gonna get hurt even more. They say twins feel things—like when the other is hurt or whatever—but let me tell you something...I never felt my brother fucking you, and that just burns me up. Why does he get to have all the fun?"

Deborah's eyes are calculating, but Arturo doesn't seem to notice, too concentrated on getting his dick wet. The sick fuck.

But I know how this ends. I just don't know the details—the stuff that was blacked out of the report given to me. It's just as bad as I feared. My wife was terrified in her last moments on this earth. And at the hands of my own flesh and bone.

The anger inside boils over, and yet there is nothing I can do about it.

I grab her shorts and yank them down her thighs, grunting like a beast. Deborah darts her eyes around, searching for the right moment. I notice this and hope she gets her chance. Arturo is too preoccupied. But what does it matter? I know how this ends. In so much blood the mattress has to be removed as biohazard waste.

I've seen the photos. All those stab wounds...

My thick fingers grab the elastic band of her underwear and rip them off.

Deborah yelps, but it is more instinctual. It is just enough to cause me to pause. She makes her move.

Deborah reaches between my legs and grabs my balls, like clasping a sack of marbles. There's a moment of shock. I suck in a startled breath at how things have changed. She yanks with all her might.

The skin is elastic and stretches like rubber, but the pain is crippling. Jolts of electricity are sent through my body and deep into my gut, like she has jammed a live wire into my pisshole. She continues to yank until the flesh reaches its breaking point.

I scream and swing at her face with all my might. The punch knocks the wind out of her sails, throwing her body back.

I breathe heavy, pain radiating from my nether regions, and grab the hunting knife Deborah tried to kill me with. It feels good and right in my hand. The punch didn't knock her out, but she is certainly seeing stars.

"You fucking stupid bitch," my mouth says. I can't stop the words, can't prevent my actions. Just a slave to my twin brother's body.

I stare down at her. The weight of my damaged testicles hangs lower than before, and they are swelling like grapefruits. Was that in the police report? Was there mention about Arturo's balls having been yanked like taffy?

What the fuck am I waiting for?

Deborah stirs some more, then shifts. Her bleary eyes rest on me. I grin despite the pain in my stomach from my stretched testicles, which makes me want to puke. Arturo wants her to know what's happening. He needs her conscious while she dies. It's personal. With her children included, there were 299 stab wounds.

I grip the hilt of the knife tighter and lift it. When I leap atop Deborah, I bring the blade down in a series of quick jabs, without attention to where it kisses her body.

She snaps out of the dazed state the punch threw her into and deflects as much as she can, earning herself lacerations to her arms and wrists. Deborah climbs higher onto the bed while I go at her with the knife, stabbing her back, her legs—anywhere I can sink steel into flesh. Blood pours out of several wounds, indicating I have severed something important, like a vein or artery. This fills me with an absurd endorphin rush.

Deborah begins to slow her fight, and this pleases me even more.

Well, it pleases Arturo.

I am in Hell, watching the worst thing I can imagine happen at my own hands.

It only gets worse, brother.

Somehow, despite my balls having been stretched like pizza dough, I have an erection. And it *hurts*. I can't understand how this is possible. With each throb of my cock, darts of pain radiate through my guts. And yet my heartbeat accelerates, and I become more fevered for something raw, something beautifully degenerate. Arturo's loathing of me pours out like a volcano erupting its hot hatred.

My chest heaves. These thoughts take hold, anger rising within. I grab Deborah's head and tilt it to the side. With the knife, I stab her in the ear, over and over again, until the last of her crying and screaming and squirming has ceased. The blade slams down hard enough to break through the skull, twisting around to create a red, wet hole.

All the while, my throbbing penis is engorged, to the point of bursting. I cram it into the hole I fashioned through her ear canal. For a moment, the warmth of her brain feels wonderful, but that is short-lived. When I extract my penis, hoping for a good couple of pumps before shooting my load into her cerebellum, something terrible happens.

The pushed-inward shards of her skull act like a trap, digging into my cock when I try to pull out. I panic and yank myself backward, ripping my member out of her fractured bone. There's no way to tell how badly I'm hurt from all the blood, but it's pouring out of me like rainwater leaking from a busted gutter. I take a few steps, my vision swooning, and slip.

My fall is quick and lethal, my head catching the edge of the bed frame. The decorative bedpost goes into my eye and through my skull.

****

Try again. Turn to page 127.

She brings the cleaver down onto Danny's head, like an axe embedding into a green log, and I turn away. I clench my eyes when the sickening noises of his body being hacked to ribbons rings out behind me. Wet sounds. Over and over. Jan speaks beneath her breath, but I cannot make out her words through the chorus of metal on meat and bone.

My act is a cowardly one, and I am very aware of that. I'm disgusted with myself, but I am also terrified for my life. Still, I know I should turn and go after her. How much damage can she do with that cleaver? Can I arrest her arm and get the blade away? If so, I could easily subdue her, but if I fail, I will become minced, just like Thomas and Danny Boy. Poor misunderstood Danny Boy. His blood is now on my hands.

Though most of Greenwood Planes will assume he fucked up and deserved his plight, I will always know the truth—the sad boy hiding behind the tough guy façade. I'm sure his parents know who he really is, and they'll blame me for bringing him into this madhouse, just as much as I blame myself.

"Now, there's twice as much to clean," Jan says. "So you better get to it."

She's finished butchering Danny, but I don't even realize it at first. I drifted off, perhaps into that very land Danny went to escape our awful situation. But I have the drive to live. To do whatever I can to get out of this. I can't allow myself to drift away like that.

She's not going to let you go.

I remind myself of this while I turn to face the granny butcher. So innocent, if you wash away the blood and remove the weapon. Or maybe not. The look on her face—wide eyes staring into nothing, mouth slightly parted, slack jaw—must have been the last thing ol' Thomas saw before he met his maker.

"What are you waiting for?" Jan asks.

My breathing escalates into something on the verge of hyperventilation. I calm myself. Take a deep breath. Swallow hard.

"I can't cut up Danny." I shake my head.

"You don't have to. I just did. Bag'em and get'em down the chute."

Reluctantly, I nod. If I can get out of this, all will be forgiven. It wasn't me, after all, who killed these two men. I'm just doing what I have to do to get out and call the law. In the end, this crazy old lady will be locked up for life. Her story will end up on *Dateline* or maybe a mini-series on Netflix.

"Where's the chute?"

"Just outside the back door in the kitchen. Each level shares a shoot that drops garbage into the dumpster below, in the garage."

I nod, eyes cast down, unable to believe what I'm about to do.

"And speed it up! Time's a wastin'. I need to clean myself up so I can finish the snacks and get the Bunco tables set up." Jan looks at her watch. "Jesus Almighty, we've got an hour and a half." She snaps her fingers. "Chop, chop!"

And I'll be damned, but like the spineless amoeba I am, I get right to it. Only this time, I slip on a pair of heavy-duty gloves—those thick yellow ones that are fiber on the inside with a coating of rubber on the outside. Using the pile of garbage liners she left for me, I begin bagging up pieces of Danny.

It's not hard work, but a painful ordeal. I put his hands into one bag and wrap it in duct tape, then his feet in another. Each leg gets its own. I try to keep the bags clean so blood doesn't transfer onto the garbage chute. But why? What do I care if blood transfers? I'm getting out of this place and calling the fucking cops. Screw the damn blood!

With that in mind, I bag quicker, just to be finished with the vile task. I almost puke. The heavy mineral odor of blood is all-consuming. I can taste it, like I have a mouthful of old pennies. There's so much. It's on everything: the throw rug, the walls, speckling the ceiling. It's even on the furniture. She's crazy to think this place will ever be in good enough shape for company in an hour and a half.

But that doesn't matter to me. Not at all.

After bagging up the corpses, I grab a couple of small bags—likely hands or feet—and make my way to the kitchen, where Jan has finished washing her hands. She missed dots of red on the backs of her arms and elbows, probably planning on taking a bath. Her face and neck are spattered, like an all-American psycho. You'd think she was a granny who had an unfortunate accident while cooking blackberry cobbler.

"Through this door?" I ask, knowing it has to be. It's the only door in the kitchen.

She nods. "Yes. Be discreet. And know I have my eyes on you, young man."

Young man?

It's one of those back doors with a window covered by a small curtain. I grab the handle, but it won't turn. The button is stuck. Even the deadbolt won't budge. I look over my shoulder. Jan is standing there at the counter, fiddling with dips and veggies on a platter.

"There a trick to unlocking this door or something?" I ask, hoping I don't sound too demanding. There's no telling what will set her off.

She glares at me. "You're a bit slow, aren't you?"

What the fuck?

"Just unlock it like any other door, dummy."

"It's stuck."

She drops the paring knife she has been using to cut veggies. "For Christ's sake, do I have to do everything around here?" Jan steps across the linoleum to where I'm standing. "I swear, I don't know what I expected, calling a number from a card left on the doorstep to the building."

Jan grabs the doorknob and shakes it. She tries the button lock and then the deadbolt.

"What the hell did you do?" she asks.

"I didn't *do* anything."

"The hell you didn't! The damn door's stuck."

"Look, I want to get rid of this stuff just as bad as you do, so why would I sabotage your door like this?"

"I swear, if you want something done, you have to do it yourself. Nobody is worth a shit these days." She jiggles the handle again, then attempts the deadbolt. "Damn thing never stuck before."

I slip back slow and easy, careful not to make a sound. Jan continues to rant while I grab the paring knife from the cutting board. The blade is wet with tomato juice.

"Must be Thomas's doing," she says. "That man isn't worth the clothes on his body." She turns. "I tell you—"

I stab her in the throat with the knife. One quick jab and I feel sick about it.

When she pulls back, the knife slides out, and blood spurts from a severed artery, nailing me in the face with a warm spray. I keel over and puke on the kitchen floor—McFish and fries in thick chunks and bile.

Jan tries to speak, but her voice gurgles on the blood now draining down her throat. She chokes on it, spitting red everywhere. The warm drops fall on my skin, and I throw up again. The rancid stench of puked-up fish and copper has me on the floor, dry heaving, wallowing in a sluice of vomit and blood.

Jan stumbles around the kitchen, her hand to her throat, but the blood rains down like a busted PVC pipe. She falls in a corner and takes deep, wet breaths, coughing.

Have you ever watched a horror movie? Seen the victim finally knock the killer down and then run without delivering the fatal blow or stab? Have you thought to yourself, *Come on, you stupid fuck, make sure she's dead?* Yeah, me too. But I just can't do it. I have to get out of this kitchen. Out of this apartment!

Problem is, I can't.

The front door is stuck. The handle won't even move, as if it has been welded in place. The windows are the same—at least the ones I've tried, the ones in the living room. I dare not return to that foul kitchen to try the backdoor again. The wetness of my shirt and smears of chewed fast food are enough of a reminder to keep me well away.

I walk down the hall. There's a bathroom to the left. I poke my head inside. It smells of Lava soap and is pristine, decorated in pink and green pastels. There are two bedroom doors, both closed.

*****

Take the door on the right. Turn to page 65.

Take the door on the left. Turn to page 131.

I choose the door on the right. Inside, I find a shrine. And, God forbid, a corpse.

Or is it a statue of some sort? Who knows.

I look behind me and down the hallway, fearing Jan will somehow get up, but a stab wound to the throat is fatal. I once cleaned a house after a homicide, a single stab to the throat. There was a lot of blood.

This room is clean and neat, but there isn't much to it outside of the shrine and a bevy of pictures on the wall. Photos and newspaper clippings. Who reads the newspaper anymore? I look closely. The date on one front page says, "June 17, 1999." Makes sense. The *Greenwood Planes Tribune* went digital years ago, due to poor sales and high costs of production.

The figure at the base of the shrine is spooky, and I can't take my eyes off him. His skin is yellow but not jaundiced. Like it's cast in resin. There does appear to be a substance over the dummy. A resin that has discolored with age.

Beneath is a human figure. A young man. The waxen statue is dressed in a track outfit too bright and clean. Behind the body are candles on a shelf adorned with trophies and medals. The dates are all from the nineties.

The bits of articles pinned to the wall indicate this figure is the representation of Jan and Thomas's son, Rickey—a high school track star who was expected to go pro and follow in his mother's footsteps. He was projected to be an Olympian and had the skill level and drive to be one of the greats. Until he was paralyzed in a car accident.

According to the articles, Rickey was released into the care of his parents.

I look at the strange figure. Stare. Wonder. I don't really understand what comes over me, but I give the figure a tap to the head.

It isn't even a *hard* hit. Almost as if I want to assure myself this isn't *really* Rickey by not tempting fate too much. But that's all it takes for the head to break free. It falls to the hardwood, and the resin shatters.

A putrid odor emanates from the neck, wet with advanced rot. The head beneath the resin is preserved on the outside but gummy where it came away from the spine. The stink is powerful, and yet I stay right where I am, staring and wondering.

They kept this secret for decades.

It was only a matter of time before one of them lost it.

Try Not to Die in This Damned House III

Feeding her was always a chore, even after all these months.

Markus had spotted her one afternoon while scanning Greenwood Planes with his telescope. He did that daily: watching people and deciding which of his buildings he wanted to torment next. Markus created the structures, but the people typically came from nearby towns and bigger cities. He charged reasonable rates, which was a great incentive for people to rent from him, despite his reputation amongst the locals of being a slumlord.

The woman walking down the street had gone to a liquor store. When she emerged after making her purchase, she held a brown bag in hand—what appeared to be a fifth. Markus had sighed at the sight, reminded of his parents and their struggles with alcohol. He watched for her, noticing she bought that same bottle every few days.

Markus pitied the woman and her vice. She was one who would not be missed, drowning in the booze she thought dulled her pain.

It was nine months ago that Markus ventured out of his house and into town. He was reluctant to do so, suffering from crippling anxiety spawned from his life in isolation. Food and any necessary supplies for his home and the models of Greenwood Planes were always delivered. The only thing to cause him to venture away from his property upon the hill was something of utmost importance, which could not be delivered directly to him.

Such as Deanne.

He learned her routine and made a trip one night after seeing her buy a bottle from the liquor store. Markus found out which apartment she lived in and made his way to the back door. Intimately familiar with said apartments, he knew how to stick to the shadows to not be seen.

Though he did not format his models with security devices, many of his tenants used Ring cameras and other such security measures. Most of the time, apartment renters weren't as attentive to their personal security as home dwellers. Deanne certainly wasn't.

Before leaving the house, Markus had removed the back door on the model apartment where Deanne lived. He used an Exacto knife to cut out the handle of the door, then replaced it on the building. Once he arrived, he was greeted with a backdoor with no handle. Markus smiled at his handiwork before looping his finger in the hole, where there should have been a doorknob, and pulled it open with ease.

He was hit with the odor of whiskey, like walking into a bar after hours. Markus had waited long enough for her to get good and drunk, and he wasn't surprised she was three sheets to the wind. With a little coaxing, he got her into his car—it was his parents' vehicle he drove on rare occasion. Markus brought her home and secured her in a room, where he had plastered over the window to create a plain white box of nothing. He had hammered heavy-duty Tapcon bolts through the concrete and fastened them with chains and cuffs. These measures had been planned and ready weeks before he kidnapped her.

Once in the room, Markus stripped her of her clothes and stared at the naked woman. He had expected to get aroused, just seeing her there in the nude, but that didn't happen. Markus was flaccid, and she was a crying, slobbering mess. She reminded him of the nights he would find his mother passed out on the couch or even the floor in the living room, head tilted to the side in a puddle of vomit.

Markus used several *Penthouse* magazines to prime himself. He had found them in a trunk in the garage years ago. Must have belonged to his father. Markus had used them before for sexual gratification, but he wasn't much into masturbation. He got his jollies off watching Greenwood Planes and fucking with people.

Once he was ready to go, he went into the room and did his best despite the smell of alcohol and vomit. He closed his eyes, picturing one of the ladies from the magazine while he raped Deanna. It was Markus's first sexual experience with a woman, so it didn't take long for him to come.

When he was finished, he held his rod inside of her quivering body while she cried. The smells and her sobs sickened him. He pulled out and left the room without so much as looking at her, repulsed with the situation but even more disgusted with himself.

Markus went back into the room every day after, forcing himself upon her. Eventually, he visited her three and four times a day. He liked doggy style best. Markus brought in a two-by-four to place between her knees, forcing her legs apart. He would grab the back of her head and push her face into the wall, pounding her like an animal, over and over, grunting and thrusting. The corner muffled her screams. Eventually, the drywall was chipped from her teeth, the paint dirtied from her sweat and tears.

He repeated this sick ritual until she began showing. And it was a good thing because Markus was getting bored with her, finding it harder and harder to orgasm.

Markus hadn't sexually assaulted her in months. He fed her three times a day, mostly by force since she was desperate to go on a hunger strike. Markus knew nothing about prenatal vitamins or any such measure for fetal health. He fed her whatever he had on hand and watched while his child grew within her womb.

Her belly was huge now. He figured she would go into labor any day, but he was scared, not knowing what to do when her water broke. Markus had been watching documentaries on childbirth for weeks in preparation.

To get his mind off how drastically his life would change once his child was birthed into the world, he focused on the fourplex apartment he was currently tormenting. Markus unscrewed the cap from a flashlight, took out the tiny bulb within, and placed it into the window of the next unit in the apartment.

Afterimage

I saw the first human shape—ghost, if you will, though I don't particularly like thinking of them that way, or at least I didn't back then—after staring too closely into the television when I was a kid.

Back then, TVs were big clunky things, often in massive oak boxes doubling as stands when they decided to stop working, upon which the next TV would be perched. It seemed everyone bought one of those huge monstrosities at some point in the eighties, only to downsize to something which fit nicely on its darkened husk.

I saw *them* in the big TV before its tube went out—or whatever it was that made those old dinosaurs go bottom-up. The TV sat on the floor, which was convenient for me since I was always down there anyway. I'd scooch closer to the thing while sorting through my baseball cards, lining them up by team or field position. Cartoons would blare in my face, and I could see the pixilation of the screen.

That's how those old TVs were, you know. If you got real close or put your eyes right up to the glass, you could make out the pattern of primary colors which translated somehow into the images we watched daily.

It was a Saturday morning, I remember that clearly. I was putting all my Donn Russ cards in one pile, the Topps cards in another, and Fleer cards in a third. It would be a few more years until Upper Deck cards came along and stole the show. I looked up at the TV, so close the image was distorted. Who even knows which cartoon it was.

I became lost in one of those strange moments, focused on something with almost no thoughts, mind completely blank, as if in a trance. Staring at that television. My mother always told me not to sit too close to the TV, that it would make me lose my sight. Turns out, it made me do some wild shit, but I never went blind.

I sat there and stared at the colors of the picture, watching it change and mutate. So close to the screen the sound, the canned laughter in the background and silly voiceovers, didn't match the images at all.

What I thought was my name was whispered, so I pivoted my head, fearing Mom caught me staring directly into the TV again. She would have been pissed, but she wasn't there. What I saw instead was an undulating green blob—what I later learned was an afterimage.

Typically, an afterimage will take on the shape of whatever you have been staring at in bright light when you turn away into darkness. But I had been gazing so closely at the television screen, and there was no distinguishable image, just a colorful blob.

I looked around the living room. The green blob was pasted over my every vision, as if a filter had been inserted in my retinas. That's when I saw the first *thing*.

It was standing beside the couch, staring at me, revealed through the strange cast of psychedelic green afterimage. There was no internet at the time, so the Tall Man did not exist yet, but that's what it looked like. No discernable face, but human in form, pale and spoiled, though it was hard to tell those details through the filter in my vision.

It raised its arm and pointed at me, and I could have died right there. I closed my eyes, shook like leaves in a windstorm, and prayed to Major League Baseball for it to go away. By the time I opened my eyes again, the afterimage was gone, right along with the creepy thing standing beside the couch. I never looked at that couch the same again. And I never sat so damn close to the TV.

I say all this because despite my curiosity getting the better of me in my youth, causing me to stare into light bulbs every now and then to see *them*, it has been a long time since I've done so. I forgot about *them*.

Until now.

There was a time when I thought about the people of the light quite a bit, fearful of their existence and the knowledge they are always around us, watching, waiting. Eventually, I realized whatever they are here for must not include me because they never did anything. They just observed and could only be located if I *really* tried to see them. If I didn't make the effort, they were out of sight, out of mind.

Life moved on, and I forgot about the people of the light. I had a string of girlfriends and dead-end jobs. Moved out of my parents' house and blazed a path in this crazy thing called adulthood. Seems like I have made just about every mistake a man can make, outside of meth or heroin addiction—I never was one for recreational drugs, though I tried pot a few times. I'm not into drinking either because I don't like the way it dulls my brain. Substances like that aren't needed to make poor decisions. I can only imagine what kind of choices I would make if I got drunk or stoned.

My problem is, I get these great ideas, and I act on them without thinking too much about the consequences. Seems like I'm always getting a car repoed, drowning in product for some stupid online pyramid scheme—of which I'm at the very bottom of—dodging calls from creditors, and eventually filing for bankruptcy.

This isn't the way my parents raised me, and they remind me of that every time I see them. That's why I don't visit them as often as they would like, not wanting to be their whipping post. I'm well aware of my misgivings, thank you very much, and in no mood to be constantly reminded of my bad decisions.

My last girlfriend told me I should see a doctor, that maybe I'm bipolar. Well, fuck that. I'm not about to be put on some drug which zaps my libido, causes me to gain weight, or turns me into a zombie. She was a decent girl, but I couldn't swing with all the talk of seeing a specialist. Soon enough, she mentioned seeing other people and here I am, alone in a shitty apartment. Again.

The loneliness doesn't bother me all that much, but it is especially difficult after a long-term relationship. It's the little things that get you: not having someone there to chat with while watching TV, no one to share meals with, going to sleep alone in a cold bed. But I'll get used to that eventually. I always do. After all, I'm forty-three now. I've had several long-term relationships, but nothing I'd put a ring on. They always leave me, and I always get over them.

These days, I wonder if I even *want* the supposed fulfillment which comes with marriage and commitment. After the initial days of depression and self-loathing because of a breakup, I always find a new lease on life. Right now, I'm in those stagnant depths, but soon enough, I will be back on my feet again.

Maybe I'll reactivate my apps and set up a few hit'em-and-quit'em romps, just for fun. Who knows?

Maybe I should call Amy.

*****

Call Amy. Turn to page 52.

Leave Amy in the past. Turn to page 83.

I put my hand on the cold doorknob and hesitate before turning it. Gabriel and Hope cry on the other side, each of their sobs easily distinguishable from one another. Do I really want to see this?

I'm having one of those moments where their little lives flash in my mind: trips to the ice cream parlor, playing catch at the park, teaching them how to ride a bike, birthday parties. A tidal wave of emotion crashes over me while I stand there, gripping the doorknob, and though I feel like crying, nothing happens. The body in which my consciousness is nestled feels nothing.

Arturo has no good memories, no family, nothing. I'm suddenly filled with his essence, like being clasped in some kind of icy grip. My heartbeat accelerates when I turn the knob. I push open the door, and something warm inside melts the ice. Foolishly, I believe it is because I see my kids crouched together under the covers in Gabriel's bed, but that isn't it at all. My consciousness feels compassion and hurt, but my body senses something different.

I walk into the room, eyes trained on the quivering form beneath Gabriel's comforter. They snivel and whimper, and despite feeling sorry for them, I chuckle. I don't want to, but I do. Or better yet, *Arturo* chuckles, and I am forced to live vicariously through his actions. I try to stop this, to save my children from their awful fate, but I am unable to do more than watch from the eyes of my twin. His evil breathes into my soul.

"Why are you hiding from Daddy?" Arturo asks.

Daddy? What the fuck?

Their cries intensify. The comforter has red smears. They're hurt, and I want desperately to help them. But the icy tethers of Arturo's mind keep my consciousness in place, helplessly watching a scene from my own personal Hell.

I grab the comforter at the foot of the bed and yank, revealing Gabriel and Hope, clutched together. My boy holds his little sister tightly, protecting her as best he can. My little hero.

My little man. I realize, not for the first time, that I will never see them grow up. Never watch them find love. Never witness them achieve success in life. Never rejoice in them reaching those milestones every father looks forward to.

"Not everyone gets to be a father," Arturo says, and I wonder if he spoke that in the moment replaying before my eyes or if he is saying that to me.

Hope buries her face into her brother's chest, her body heaving from deep sobs. Gabriel stares me in the eyes with an intensity I have never seen from him. In that moment, my little boy became a man, if only for the final minutes of his life.

"Why are you doing this, Dad?" he asks, and my heart breaks.

It's not me! It's not your dad!

He can't hear my words. Only Arturo's were spoken on that evening, when Deborah and I had a fight and I left. When I wasn't there to protect my family.

"Daddy doesn't love you anymore."

You bastard!

The look in Gabriel's eyes dissolves into a crushed child. Those words are worse in that moment than death, being told his father does not love him anymore. He shakes his head, and tears cascade down his cheeks afresh.

Hope shifts and faces me. "Please, Daddy! Please don't hurt me!"

I would cut my own throat rather than witness this. No police report could have prepared me for the emotional sting of this twisted reality. How could my own flesh and blood do this to me?

My fingers grip the knife in my hand tighter. My adrenaline is heightened, and I know what is coming next. I want nothing to do with it, and yet I cannot turn away, unable to do anything but live through my brother's depraved actions.

He moves us closer to the bed. My children back into the wall, as if they can push themselves through and escape this terrifying situation.

"No, Daddy, no!" Hope sobs.

"Oh yes." It's Arturo, but it *feels* like I'm saying those words. "You see, Daddy can't have a couple of disappointments like you in his life." I shake my head, feel the smile on my lips. "Nope. You're good for nothing. You make me feel sad. Nothing you do makes me proud. Your artwork on the fridge is shit. I tell you I like it, but I lie. I *hate* it." My shins and knees touch the bed. "I hate both of you. I want you to know that. I want you to think about that while I'm killing you—how much I hate you."

They are both crying messes, too ashamed to even look at me.

You fucking asshole! I can't believe this! You're a goddamned monster.

"Am I?"

I lunge forward onto the bed, knife held high. The blade swishes through the air, and I drive it into Gabriel's legs in a staccato motion, then into Hope's squirming calves and feet. They kick, but the blade bites into their tender flesh so easily, so effortlessly.

Their screams grow loud and strained. They try to escape, but I stab, keeping them in place. Like a knife in a side of beef, the blade enters Hope's thigh with a meaty punch, then makes a sucking noise when I pull it out and slam it into Gabriel's calf while he tries to launch himself onto the floor.

"You're not getting away, you little shits," I say with Arturo's voice. In his excitement, his tone doesn't resemble mine as much as it has, but I doubt my kids recognize that in their struggles.

I pull the knife free from Gabriel's calf, and he falls in a loud thump on the hardwood. Hope tries to dash off the bed on the opposite side, but I catch her shoulder with the blade, jabbing it through to the hilt and yanking her body toward me. I clutch her in my arm, pull the blade out, and stab her in the chest several times. She slumps over on the bed with the occasional twitch—the final spasms of her nerves firing off.

Gabriel crawls across the floor, leaving a smear of blood, like a big red snail. I feel the smile, and I hate every second of it. Arturo has been happy while murdering my family. The cold I have felt since entering his consciousness is replaced by the fires of Hell.

Just when I slide off the bed, the door opens and Deborah comes into the room like a rabid banshee. Her battle cry towers over the sobs of our son. In her hand is a trophy I was given at work for Employee of the Year. She holds it by the decorative end and attempts to use the heavy marble base like a mallet. Deborah runs up on me and swings. I am fast and mostly dodge her attempt but get nailed in the shoulder.

With a yelp, I swing the knife, but she is quick with the trophy clutched in both hands. She swats my arm so hard, the marble snaps my wrist, causing the knife to fling away. Pain screams from the point of impact, only matched by anger like I've never experienced before.

Inside, my heart breaks for Deborah. Consumed with guilt, I feel a mountain of shame for not being there. It never would have come to this. I would have been able to do something had Arturo come by while I was home, even if I had to physically restrain him while she called the police.

"You fucking asshole!" she yells. I can't tell if she's yelling at Arturo or me. Does she know it isn't me?

With my right hand out of commission, I reach forward with the left, aiming for her throat, but she dodges and leaps on top of me, catching me by surprise. I fall backward, hitting the hardwood with a boom so loud I'm surprised we didn't break through the floor and end up in the crawl space beneath.

Though I struggle to free myself, the pain radiating from my head causes a wave of dizziness to cloud my vision. Deborah uses her nails to slash at my face. I scream and try to get away, but she is like a feral animal. Her motherly instincts allow her to tap into something primal, which she unleashes on me, her teeth gritted, grunts and strangled cries escaping while she claws my eyes out.

The last thing I see is her face—so unlike the gentle, loving one I am used to—replaced with a mix of terror and fury. Everything goes black. Pain sears through my eye sockets and into my brain. I continue to struggle blindly, and Deborah continues to tear me to shreds.

Her fingernails are like razors on my arms and legs, and then she grabs my throat, sinking her nails in deep and squeezing with all her might. I struggle to breathe.

The pain is all-consuming.

***

Try again. Turn to page 127.

"How is it we can't afford groceries and yet you buy that stuff for your hair?" I ask.

It's an honest question met with a bitter response, which I should have seen coming.

"Gary, I swear to God. If there is anything that gives me pleasure in this life, you will do anything you can to squash it."

I sigh. "Tanya, it isn't like that."

"I swear." Her teeth clench, the nagging voice penetrating their enamel barrier. "Don't push me, Gary. Don't you even think about it."

"What color is it this time?"

I can't help myself. Tell an old dog not to push, and that's exactly what he's going to do.

"Let me guess," I say. "Blue. Did you finally get blue hair dye so you can fit in with those old biddies you play cards with? Like that lady next door. What'ser name?"

"Keep it up, Gary."

"Or maybe you got red this time, to match your fiery attitude."

"How about black to match the color of your heart," she says.

I'm taken aback, and that's when I get a glimpse of the sheers in her hand. They swing around from behind and lodge in my throat.

***

The correct choice was Keep my mouth shut.
Turn to page 8.

How many nights have I gazed upon the butchered bodies of my family? Am I looking for some clue as to Arturo's motive, or am I just a glutton for punishment? The memory of my wife and children fades while I spend more and more time with these morbid photos. I cannot even remember what their smiles looked like. All I know is blood and disfigurement, bodies strewn in ways which accounted for abuse after death.

Arturo was a sick fuck. I think we all knew that from an early age, but no one wanted to address it or get him help. It was almost as if having a twin made it easier to forget about him.

Now, I can never do that. He is etched into my mind with more permanence than the connective tissue of sharing our mother's womb.

A sound pulls me from my obsession with the police reports. It's coming from down the hall. A sure sign it's time for me to go to bed. My mind is acting up again.

I stand, and the sound comes again, but I cannot make out what it is. Ecstasy or agony. Something about it beckons. I have spent so much time in the tiny apartment that I have every noise memorized: every creaking floorboard, every adjusting corner from settlement, every whoosh of wind rattling loose windowpanes. Everything.

But this sound...

It is human but monstrous in its permuted renderings, like someone with a microphone crammed down their throat and plugged into an amplifier with an odd mix of effects. And it's more than one. I also hear...young voices modulated and mixing with one another.

Behind them is another sound, like helicopter propellers swooshing in slow motion. A whirring in rhythm with my heartbeat.

A feeling of comfort swells, enveloping me. I'm incredibly tired but simultaneously curious about what I am hearing from down the hallway.

*****

Ignore the sounds and get some sleep.
Turn to page 124.

Investigate the sound. Turn to page 17.

*****

Don't get the wrong idea here. I'm a bachelor at the moment, but not a slob. I keep my place tidy. Always have, even in the dark times such as this. No leaning tower of pizza boxes stacked in the corner next to the garbage can, no dishes in the sink. And my bed is always made. I might struggle with commitment and jumping after every shiny thing I see, but that doesn't mean I'm a pig. Quite the contrary.

The one vice I do have is smoking. It's nasty, I know, but there's nothing like a lungful of tobacco smoke early in the morning. That initial drag off a fresh ciggy is like nothing else. It's all downhill from there. I swear, I live for that first one, and I enjoy the hell out of it every fucking morning. By the time I'm taking the last one of the night, my lungs burn, and it tastes like shit, but I know the first drag of the next day will be a delight.

The other day, I took that sweet pull of freshly sizzling tobacco and held it in, yearning for the lightheadedness I remember from when I was a teenager. It's long gone, but I remember. Now it's a sense of being fixed. An almost tingly feeling of satisfaction I must chase all day long, like a fiend. I tilted my head back, savoring the full flavor and wondering how it was that some people didn't perform this very ritual every goddamned morning of their life like I do.

When I opened my eyes, I was looking straight into a light in the ceiling. My initial response was to cringe, but I had a strange moment there. I opened my eyes wider and stared into the light. Smoke dissipated against the ceiling.

For a moment, I was transported to a simpler time, before I knew the satisfaction of cigarettes. A time when I would stare at a light to escape the talk of my uncle dying of cancer in the hospital. To get away from the tears, the regret, the remorse. An all-enveloping light blotting all sadness around me, if only for a few minutes.

My life is a really bad place. I cannot see up from here, but I assure myself there *is* an up to be seen, that I'm not in some topsy-turvy world, spinning wheels and getting nowhere fast.

Though I'm depressed, I'm managing. Smoking more, yes, but that's to be expected, right? In a bad, bad place, where something as simple as searing light into my retinas and being reminded of a vice prior to the cigs has given me temporary solace.

I finally took a deep breath and looked away from the light, amazed, for a moment, at the massive afterimage in bluish green pulsating before my eyes. My mind throbbed with my heartbeat, continuing in a steady *thump* at the base of my neck. I looked around through the blob of an afterimage, spotting something sitting on my couch.

Some*one*.

For a split-second, I thought Amy had come back to me, but no, despite the familiarity of the figure, it wasn't her at all.

The featureless form craned its head toward me, its skin gray and dead. It said, "We've been waiting for you."

I stared, frozen in place. My heartbeat so loud I could hear it. I didn't take a breath for minutes while the afterimage faded. And with it, the unsettling visage of one of *them*, the people of the light.

*

That was yesterday, but I'm in no better of a place today. I call off from work, feigning an illness. After Covid, it is the easiest way to get the administration to give me a few days off, no questions asked.

I stare at the couch, wondering if *they* are looking at me. Can *they* do anything to me through the ethers? I don't think so, or those things would be doing shit to people all the time, right?

There's a theory life exists in a single moment into perpetuity—infinitesimal things having happened, happening, and going to happen in that single moment, imprinted on the fabric of reality. No actual past or future, just a present always happening, always recorded. It's an odd theory which makes no sense to me, but having been given a glimpse into some inner dimension has me thinking about such things.

After chain-smoking several cigarettes, I decide I have to see them again. I stand on a chair to get up close and personal to the light in the ceiling. The outside is sticky with years of accumulated tar. Just like my lungs. I stare into the light while I focus on my breathing.

The way my lungs feel, I smoke too much, but I just can't stop, especially not now. I *want* to, but I can't. The brightness is all-consuming, until it is my everything, until I find it difficult to think about other things, like smoking and Amy. She wanted me to stop because she isn't a smoker. I never can understand how someone who is not a smoker ends up with someone who is.

Flashes of color erupt in my brain, like brilliant haloes out of the stark white enveloping the entirety of my vision. Thoughts drift away into the recesses, swallowed by the strange folds in reality. A sensation like being in a whirring vacuum starts at the top of my spine and travels up my neck, nestling within my brain.

It is time.

I pull my face away from the ceiling light, suddenly assaulted by a typhoon of dizziness. The wobbly chair I am perched upon gives, and I tumble to the floor with a loud *boom*, which certainly was felt throughout the quadplex. Because I manage to catch the brunt of the fall with my shoulder and torso, my head is only tapped.

I lie there, wondering what the hell has gotten into me to make me do something so stupid. Here I am, staring into lights again, like when I was a kid. If only someone saw me on the chair, with my face plastered to the ceiling light fixture, I would be taken in for psychiatric care for sure.

A blooming afterimage, like tiny fireworks, explodes in my brain. This needs to stop before it gets out of hand. I'm too old for this shit. Yes, I'm in a rough patch, but I will get through it, just like every other time. It's a part of life. I can do this. I—

A form materializes out of nothing, standing over me, craning its head to look down on me. Its skin is so pale, so gray, so lifeless, like a figure molded of drab clay. Only, it moves in a curious manner, as if frames of its existence are missing. Shifty movements becoming tangled in my turbulent mind.

The fear creeps in like some unwanted sensation, the very antithesis of the feeling when you fall for a beautiful woman. It observes me, faceless. Blinking, colorless eyes. Is it curious? Frustrated? Angry?

I cannot tell.

It reaches for me. Its hand is featureless, like a mannequin's appendage, yet textured like something long dead. I tremble, caught in that moment as if trapped in a night terror. Its fingertips touch my face. Cold, stiff fingertips, like shafts of ice.

A shiver ripples through my body at its touch, and I detect, for a fleeting moment, an expression on its face. The touch does exactly the opposite for the featureless being. It seems to feel something of ecstasy in my agony.

The afterimage drifts away, and with it the being of the light.

But the cold chill of its fingers lingers on my face, almost as if something has been imprinted upon me in that terrifying moment.

I lie there, breathing hard, shaking, sweating.

And for some fucking reason I cannot explain, despite the fear gripping my aching heart, I want to see more of that thing.

**

In the days following, I swear they are watching me. I only get fractures of a glimpse, just from the corner of my eye, as if they're stealthily spying, waiting for some opportunity which never presents itself. Perhaps they're waiting for me to make the next move.

The lights entice me. Even the television—any light source, for that matter. I wonder if I can see them whenever I want, merely by filling my vision with blinding light. I want to, but also, I am frightened. There's something nefarious about them, the way they linger just outside my vision, watching.

I try to speak with them, but I look like an insane man talking to nothing in a lonely apartment. Amy hasn't lived with me, not yet at least. We talked about it many times, but it just didn't work out that way. Maybe she knew for some time she was going to leave me. Maybe that was why she was so reluctant to take things to the next level. I should have seen it.

When my thoughts drift to Amy and our failed relationship, that's when I notice one of *them* in the shadows. The more aware I become, the more I try to locate them, but they always vanish when I so much as shift, always knowing exactly when I am going to look in their direction. The feeling like they are creeping up on me is terrifying. Knowing I cannot see them has me shifty, like someone on a days-long meth binge.

The news and social media have been non-stop coverage of the coming solar eclipse, as if it's some monumental event possibly resulting in a catastrophic alteration to life as we know it. Warnings of traffic jams, low inventory at grocery stores, a slight shift in the economy due to so many people taking the day off work...Crazy stuff. It will be here and over in a matter of minutes, all this absurd coverage forgotten about. But for now, the constant public outcry mingles with my own thoughts of Amy and *them*.

So much on my mind. Amy hasn't tried to call, and why should she? I have held the phone in my hands no less than a dozen times, finger poised to hit the send button, entire messages deleted before lobbing an ill-fated text. I'm sick, and I'm hurting.

What I need is something to take my mind off of my heartache, and cigarettes only do so much to patch a hemorrhaging heart.

I have one of those LED flashlights that were all the rage for a minute there. Remember those? The little ones every man got in his stocking or as a gift when no one knew what to give him? At one time, I must have had five of them. I probably gave my father and uncles a few for birthdays and Christmas. I mean, sometimes the package came with a fold-out knife or tire gauge or something. And wow, were those lights bright! It was such a nuisance to have one aimed at your eye, often by a toddler or devious little nephew who found one of the many unwrapped that year around the Christmas tree.

Yeah, I still have one, I know it.

In the kitchen, I search the junk drawer and hit pay dirt. Two LED flashlights, completely forgotten about but there in case of an emergency. This isn't one, but it would be, perhaps, a good distraction from my ex.

Without thinking too much about it, I flick both lights on—one is on some pulse setting, taking no less than five clicks of the button to get a steady beam—and put them over my eyes. At first, I keep them closed, the brightness of the LED light glowing through my eyelids. With a few deep breaths, I open my eyes and stare into the blinding beams.

A sear radiates through my retinas and directly into my brain. It's so bright, like nothing I can explain. The throbbing pulses while I ride this strange flash of lightning. Colors in bright explosions swirl like an oil slick, minus the black. Blinding, painful light blotting everything out.

I remain like this for how long, I cannot tell. As long as I can take. We are all told how damaging LED light is when applied directly to your retina. It is quite apparent in the headache I suffer almost immediately. But it is more than that. It's the feeling of someone easing a red-hot shaft of iron through my skull.

Finally, I remove the lights and drop them onto the floor. When I blink my eyes, I am shocked to find I can't see anything. Not one thing. Just white. And strange, discombobulated shapes of color floating through the air.

"Oh fuck. You did it now." I stumble around my apartment like Frankenstein's monster, fresh after a lightning bolt rejuvenation.

The vague shapes of my furniture begin to come into focus, drowning in the brightness of eyes on the verge of nothingness. The figure again, only more clearly this time. He is thin and gray and sickly, featureless but clearly looking directly at me. Is it some kind of ESP between us which assures me his attention is focused on me? I'm not sure.

He's naked, his body in a state of melting or rotting away. The figure is cadaverous but unlike the dead on Earth. It's more like a suspension of animation. Like he's caught somewhere between death and life and his flesh doesn't quite know how to respond.

He reaches one arm out and gestures to me. His mouth opens, and it looks like his lips are sticking together by fused skin. The empty eye sockets are shaped in a downcast way, indicating sadness.

His finger flicks in and out, beckoning to me from the kitchen.

*****

Turn away from the stranger. Turn to page 90.

Follow the strange man into the kitchen. Turn to page 112.

I turn away from the ghastly figure and close my eyes. My vision doesn't change, as if the intense brightness is now stuck with me. Have I done permanent damage? All my childhood, I was warned about sitting too close to the TV, warned not to look directly into the sun, warned not to shine lights in my eyes.

But warnings only work on the obedient. It's easy to forget such directives in the face of something truly extraordinary, even something as frightening as what I am dealing with.

I eventually open my eyes again, and though everything looks foggy and opaque, I can make out my surroundings enough to rest assured I will regain my vision. After a moment, my focus sharpens.

A hand creeps from behind and caresses my face with its scathing, bony knuckles. I shudder and recoil, shifting my head. What phantasmal form has greeted me in such an intimate manner?

The strange man of the light, but only faintly. The sad hollows on his face, the stretched skin, like a turkey too long in the oven.

"So warm," he says. His visage fades.

**

In the hours following what I have convinced myself were strange visions brought on by overstimulating my brain through the windows of my eyes, I develop a headache like no other. Again, I assume it is a consequence of shining bright LED light directly into my retinas.

I sit in my living room with the television on, just like any other night, only things peer out of the shadows at me. Like before, I cannot see, but more or less *feel* their presence. In the corners of my eyes, they stealthily sneak into my world, previously unbeknownst to me. A constant movement until that very moment I make any effort to actually see them clearly.

It's maddening. Perhaps a sign I am losing my shit. Maybe a symptom of my loneliness?

In the melee of what happened, I *did* forget about Amy for the duration. In its own bizarre way, that was kind of nice. It's difficult losing the one you love, especially when she is the one you thought you would spend the rest of your life with. I haven't bought a ring yet, but I have been looking.

It was foolish of me to think what we had was special. She told me the breakup was a long time coming. How did I not see the signs? How was I so stupid to believe Amy felt the same way I do? *Did!* It would have been an even worse breakup had I proposed and she declined. That would have been crushing. I think about us and weep, craft several text messages, delete each one before sending. They are desperate, sad ramblings of a broken man. All the while, I smoke.

The things of the light taunt me, like sneaky cats waiting to pounce. I ignore them, then turn off the light in the kitchen and in the living room. *They* aren't as prevalent, though the glow of the television seems to bring them closer to me.

Whereas they peeked out of nooks and corners on the other side of the lighted room, they now materialize right beside me in the illuminated space just in front of the TV. And still, I cannot look directly at them without each ghostly image atomizing into nothing, only to be replaced the moment my thoughts drift to Amy.

You would think utter darkness would be terrifying in such a moment, when a host of ghosts are prying at the outer edges of my sanity, but you would be wrong—at least in this case. They seem to be attracted to light or perhaps revealed by it. Darkness brings peace from *them*, which in turn allows my mind to obsess over Amy.

She said things weren't working out, whatever that means. That we were drifting apart. I don't see that at all. She said she needs time to think. How much time, Amy?

I can't sleep. The stark darkness surrounding me is like a deep chasm of guilty ponderings and regret. It is as if all my thoughts are able to escape my mind and hover around me in the depths of my abysmal apartment.

I decide to stalk her socials once again. The glow of my phone sears into my eyes, reminding me what I did with the LEDs. My eyes adjust quickly, the glow of my phone the only source of light in the house. My home screen assures me the weather will be clear and warm tomorrow. A quick newsflash reminds me of the forthcoming eclipse.

Amy's socials reveal nothing of use. No sad song recollections or depressive ponderings on life. No posts of depression. Nothing to indicate our relationship left any sort of lasting impression on her or that she is regretful for leaving me.

I feel worse than I did when clouded with my own thoughts.

Perhaps I can go to PornHub for some relief, but I don't feel it. I continue to read Amy's posts, analyzing them for a scrap of hope, but there's nothing there.

They watch me, outside the glow of my phone. My skin crawls. They will go away once I turn my phone off, but it is unsettling to know they are there in the first place. Always watching from some hidden plane.

Without looking directly at them, I try to observe, like analyzing someone on the sly. Their faces are indistinct but human in nature. Their eyes are dark hollows staring incessantly. Their mouths hang open and yet smile while they watch, as if they are savoring my fear.

"What do you want from me?" I whisper.

One of them licks its lips with a dry, gangrenous tongue which does nothing to moisten them, the sound like a finger against sandpaper. This action causes a deep ripple of a shudder to cascade down my back and up my arms. I turn off the phone, and the darkness sweeps *them* away from me, if only till I finally fall asleep.

**

I wake with a headache. Sleep was riddled with fits and bursts. My fragmented dreams were mostly of Amy. And *them*. She invaded my mind for obvious reasons, but what about *them*? Why were they there? Maybe because they were on my mind a lot yesterday?

After a yawn so deep it almost throws my back out, I remove myself from bed and slip down the hallway. I stand at the toilet, releasing what seems like gallons of urine.

Their presence drifts like an icy mist around me. The sensation is unnerving, and I'm assaulted by a jerking shiver, which causes me to fling the final drops of yellow dew. I shake the morning offering to the John. Some of it gets on my shorts. I sigh. It'll dry.

I put coffee on, just like any other morning. But something is different. Maybe it's a feeling of freedom, a result of my separation from the girl I thought I would marry. But it's not elation or independence, like I have my life back and can do whatever I want. It isn't that because I wasn't lacking it in my life, not something I craved.

I loved Amy, could see us together forever, as sappy as that sounds. And believe me, I understand just how saccharine shit like that comes off as, but it's true. I fell hard for her, and getting back up after such a fall is proving to be more difficult than I expected.

But that's not the feeling. Not at all. Those thoughts are becoming more internalized. It's like being watched. Like when you're sleeping and someone is watching you. You wake up, not with a start, but slowly, as if you know someone is there even though you have been unconscious. It's like that. And it's happening right now.

I know it's *them*, but I have no idea how to combat this. After all, I allowed *them* back into my life, and they won't leave.

An eerie sense of cold embraces me when I walk into the living room, as if I'm forging my way through frozen fog. All the while, soft touches, the very faintest fingertips, glide across my skin. And with those subtle caresses come far away whispers, indecipherable and yet with a cadence suggesting strange promises.

By the time I sit on the couch, I'm chilled and terrified. My coffee is hot but does nothing to combat the frigid feeling surrounding me. The thermostat says it's plenty warm, and yet it feels like I'm living in a walk-in refrigerator.

"Go away," I say.

I know why I'm cold. They are watching me. It's their death-chill causing me distress. Just the thought of these pale souls has me on edge. Maybe they're always around us and I've somehow opened the door. I don't know, but I don't like it.

Maybe they're trapped in here with me. Maybe I need to get out of the house, get some sun.

When was the last time you were out of the house?

I haven't left the house in days. Haven't been eating much either. I just don't have an appetite. No motivation. Until now. A glance at one of my windows shows me it's sunny outside. Of course it is. My phone told me so. Sunny enough the solar eclipse later will be amazing.

The desire to go outside seizes me like the cold hands of death. Or are the cold hands of death seizing to keep me inside? I shake off the strange sense of doubt and make my move to the front door, eager for some sunshine. It's a feeling I haven't had in days. Not since Amy broke up with me.

I grab the handle and shake it, feeling foolish when it doesn't turn because I haven't disengaged the lock. Problem is, even with it unlocked, the handle will not turn.

"What the fuck?"

I try and try, but it will not budge. Around me, a crowd of spirits lean in. They press against my back like frozen meat and peek around my shoulders, as if pleasantly surprised I cannot leave the apartment. Their frigid presence is stifling, even though I cannot feel them physically.

How long have I stood here, staring at the front door? At the handle? Shivering like an old woman in the produce section of a grocery store?

When I stare like this in silence and complete solitude, they make themselves clearer, creeping further from the shadows. Their ethereal bodies undulate like visions from the ebbing waves of a psychedelic trip. I make no attempt to see them straight on. It's something I cannot do. They won't allow it. I stare at the doorknob, simultaneously fearful of the isolation and giddy for the distraction from Amy.

How long I stand here is anyone's guess. By the time I turn from the door and walk back into the living room, I am shivering so violently I look like I suffer from extreme palsies. I curl up with a blanket on the couch and fall asleep. The people of the light hover around me, like gnats on a rotting banana.

******

It is somewhere around one in the afternoon when I wake with a start. I cannot remember the last time I fell asleep on the couch like that. And not for such a duration. Excessive sleeping is as much a sign of depression as overeating, but I don't think I'm depressed.

I'm all clammy beneath the blanket. Like I've slept through another night. A look at my phone and I'm reminded the solar eclipse starts very soon. But I couldn't get out of my apartment earlier.

That's ridiculous, though. How could my front door get so jammed I can't even leave? I fling away the sweaty blanket and bound across the hardwood. Am I subconsciously trying to be quicker than *them*? Perhaps. But I don't admit as much to myself. That would be crazy. They don't exist except in my mind, right?

My hand hovers over the door handle, and I am suddenly paralyzed with fear. What if I cannot open it? What will I do then?

They don't want you to leave, don't you see? They want you here with them.

I decide against trying the front door. If I don't, I will never know, and that's fine with me. This is a small win in the battle against *them*. I step away from the door.

They swarm around me like cold winds, patting me with strange chills which vanish upon delicately caressing my flesh. It's everything I can muster to pretend I'm not concerned about them, but the truth is, their presence drives me nuts.

For the next few hours, I sit in front of the TV, watching information about the upcoming solar eclipse. I'm in an area that will have total coverage. Normally, this is something I would be excited about, but I am presently in a state of duress, considering what I have to deal with.

It would almost be acceptable if they were sitting here, watching TV with me, but the glow seems not to attract them so much as bring them out, brighten their presence. They stand around, staring at me expectantly, like salivating dogs. It's creepy. Every once in a while, I shift my gaze in an attempt to catch one off guard, but it vanishes each time, only to be replaced as soon as my attention is elsewhere. It becomes a game, but not one that I particularly enjoy.

At the window a few hours later, I stare out at all the people grouped outside with special glasses and good cheer. The sky is getting dark, with the moon approaching the sun. From my apartment, I have a good view. Down below is Jan, the sweet old lady from next door. But not that guy downstairs, whose family was murdered. He's been depressed. Maybe he sees ghosts too.

I watch the people outside while the sky darkens. They look up with their sunglasses. ZZ Top plays in my head, clear as day, which makes me giggle for the first time since Amy left me. And that is the only time I have thought of her since I woke up. I remember the LED lights and wonder if I should stare into the solar eclipse.

*****

Stare into the solar eclipse. Turn to page 128.

Turn away from the window. Turn to page 98.

Bang on the window for help. Turn to page 18.

I turn away from the window. The darkness of the eclipse envelopes me. I can't so much hear as *feel* a collective sigh from the people of the light. It's a disappointment I can intimately relate to. Like the despondency of your true love breaking things off.

In that strange connection with the people of the light comes a sudden urge to expose my eyes to the blinding torture of the eclipse. It's absurd, I know, but I have nothing. I can give them what they want.

But I don't really know what *it* is they want. It has something to do with looking into the light. Exposing them to me. Revealing them so they can tell or show me why they have crowded me with their presence.

When I turn to the window, it is too late. The darkness is fading, the moon passing the sun. I stare up at the spectacle those outside have been waiting weeks for but feel no pain. Brightness washes the color out of everything in my peripherals, like old Polaroids of a time lost.

But it's not enough. I look away.

The people of the light still hide in the shadows. That's what it is. They cower in the dark spots. The nooks and crannies of an illuminated world. They reveal themselves in the glow of those strange green and blue afterimages, as if I am then privy to some other world, a hidden plane of spectral existence. And they're all around me like I'm some kind of beacon.

The afterimage from staring at the shifting eclipse lingers, imprinted on my retinas. The people of the light are more visible. Something about them continues to frighten me—the eager anticipation, like a vulture tracking a dying animal.

I close my eyes, and the green halo of the sun dances in the darkness of my mind. But I also see *them*.

Terrified they have somehow invaded my thoughts, I open my eyes. They are all around me. The afterimage of the sun persists. It isn't going away. I have done permanent damage.

That means *they're* not going away.

I begin to hyperventilate, and that excites *them*.

"What the fuck do you want?"

I sound like a madman, but no one but *them* can hear me, so it doesn't matter, does it? If you are insane in your apartment and there's no one there to see, are you really insane?

No answer. Just cavernous hollow eyes staring upon me. Open mouths gaping like hungry infants waiting to suckle Mommy's breast. They want me. I know this, but I do not understand in what capacity and why they don't come after me.

What I do know is, I cannot stand to see them any longer.

Everywhere I move, they are there. They watch expectantly. I want to understand what they're waiting for, but then again, I don't. Whatever it is, it can't be good.

"We want *you*," one says in a voice like pond slime.

"We want your flesh." Another speaks in a gurgle.

"Your blood."

"Your warmth."

"We're so, so cold."

That last voice sounds desperate.

I move through my house, searching for something specific which eludes me. They do not leave me alone. Now they can speak to me freely, they exercise this right, filling my brain with whispers and chattering nonsense, diminishing my train of thought.

Whatever it is I need is not in the living room. I check the dining table in the little alcove. Nothing there. I turn and enter the kitchen.

There it is in the perpetual glowing afterimage of the sun, which is stamped on my retinas like a brand on a meat cow.

The knives!

I grab a paring knife from the block. It's all I need. A butcher knife would be overkill, and a fileting knife is too unwieldy.

"I'm sick of you fuckers!" I raise the knife gripped in my hand, like holding a candle at a vigil.

The people of the light watch. At that moment, they cannot touch me, and I cannot touch them. They are a presence, a force of nature manipulating me into breaking the barrier protecting us from one another. Though, I suspect there isn't much I can do to harm them, but much they can do to me.

It is too late. I'm not even sure there is anything I could have ever done. With *them* hanging around and whispering into my ears...I can't live like this. I grip the knife white-knuckle tight—I read somewhere blood can be quite a lubricant and cause the handle to become slick—and I drive the pointy tip of the paring knife into my left eye.

The pain is immeasurable and unlike anything I have felt before. The orb collapses, and everything goes black, like a light has been turned off. I poise the knife for the right eye, and they collectively gasp, which would have been humorous under other circumstances. As if having ethereal visitors could ever be a bit of comic relief.

I jab my other eye to the same effect. Searing pain shoots into my brain like long, thin needles, and then the lights are out. Total blackness. Nothing but the sounds of my apartment. None of *them* whispering. None of *them* visible in my mind. Nothing at all, except for the powerful odor of blood.

The warm wetness runs down my face and drips onto the hardwood floor. And hot, searing pain—like glowing coals have been placed in my damaged eye sockets. I wonder, absurdly in that moment, what the landlord will think, but he's some freak who lives in that big house up on the hill. Why worry about what he's going to think when I should be worried about getting to the hospital?

Despite the pain, I fumble my way into the living room and sit on my couch. I breathe deeply. Waves of nausea, probably due to blood loss or maybe even damage to my optic nerves, cripple my stomach. I try to collect my thoughts, but they seem to be spilling out of the weeping holes in my face.

I laugh. That's all I can do. Or am I crying?

I fumble around for my phone and dial 911.

The good thing is, I have a lot more to worry about than my recent breakup with Amy.

Try Not to Die in This Damned House IV

The scream rang out sometime in the middle of the night, jolting Markus from sleep.

It was time.

He didn't rush out of bed like an expectant father whose wife tells him her water broke, scrambling for the car keys and the overnight bag. No, he calmly removed himself from bed and yawned, a bit perturbed to be risen at such an ungodly hour. But Markus was eager to see his heir into the world. He hoped for a boy but would accept a girl, if that's what fate had in store for him. Not that Markus was a believer in fate. He was a *maker*.

He glided his feet into slippers, pondering a tugging urge to go into the attic and see if anything had happened in the apartment where he placed the little knife—the one he'd made himself from a paperclip he'd flattened into a blade. Markus used black thread for a handle. It looked like a miniature butcher knife.

Deanna let out another ripping scream, which sounded more painful than anything. Markus wasn't concerned with her well-being or her level of comfort, but he was worried about the baby. Deanna was nothing. Just a surrogate for his offspring. He would be glad to have her out of the way once the baby was born, though he might have to keep her there for breastfeeding.

Markus decided against a peek at the apartment with the knife treatment. He veered away from the stairs to the attic and into the room without any windows. The carpet around Deanna was awash in blood, as were her legs and pubis. She noticed him and screamed. The look in her eyes was one of pure hatred. Markus, taken aback, stood there like an idiot, not knowing what to do.

Why so much blood?

He didn't think there would be anything bloody about water breaking, at least not from what he'd researched about childbirth. Maybe a pinkish tint to the fluid, but not deep red like this.

"You fucking asshole!" Deanna screamed. "I fucking *hate* you."

She balled her fists and beat on her stomach repeatedly. Blood oozed from between her legs. The taut flesh surrounding her womb was lumpy and misshapen, indicating she'd snapped and began punching herself before Markus came into the room. Her screams weren't from her water breaking or contractions.

"Stop it!" Markus said.

Deanna shook her head in quick, jerking movements. "Fuck you. You're not going to have my kid. I won't allow that."

Another barrage of punches to her swollen belly, her teeth clenched tight, tears streaming down her face.

"You're hemorrhaging. You'll...You'll kill the baby."

"Good!"

She laid into her stomach even harder. More blood ran from her vaginal canal and into the crimson pool she sat in.

299 Stab Wounds

The problem with living in the very fourplex where it happened is that the memories linger. The good ones are always welcome, but tragedy has a way of pervading. Some say I'm obsessed. I can't find any evidence to the contrary, but I'd like them to stand in my shoes and do better.

While I would move out, I can't. I don't mind breaking the lease. It's just I don't have the money to rent elsewhere. I'm on a fixed income which barely pays for my rent and bills, especially after what happened. Since the incident, I've kind of become a shut-in, the ghosts of my past haunting me.

Maybe I'm foolish for spending so much time in the very apartment where it happened. Perhaps I'm torturing myself. This could be my penance for not being there that night.

The crime scene was horrible, from what the cops told me. Blood everywhere. They wouldn't let me in until the investigation was finished. They told me it would have been cruel. Maybe they are right. It could be I'm a spiritual masochist for living here after. Perhaps I was wrong to finagle my way into getting a copy of the police reports and crime scene photos. I said it was for closure, but I'm beginning to doubt my own intentions.

Maybe I'm torturing myself out of shame.

Deborah was killed in our room and the kids in theirs, but I've read the police reports. The slaughter began in the living room. Blood trails led to the bedrooms, as if my family took sanctity in their most private spaces after the attack.

I look around the apartment. The crime scene clean-up crew did a bang-up job removing the blood and painting the walls before I was allowed back. A Go Fund Me was set up for my hotel stay while the apartment was under investigation. The story didn't go viral or anything, but our little town of Greenwood Planes came through, donating enough to cover the hotel room and groceries for a while.

The police reports lie scattered on the dining room table situated in a little alcove across from the kitchen. I sit there and stare at the photographs of my dead wife and kids, read through the statements made by the police, pore over the details, as if I will find some sanctuary in there somewhere. As if, somehow, I can decode the senseless act and bring them back.

I often stand in the entry, staring into the living room, where my twin brother blew his brains out. There is no trace of what he left behind, as if it never happened.

**

Was it jealousy? Probably. It isn't like I can ask Arturo why he did it. They say twins have the ability to feel when the other is in danger, that some of them finish one another's sentences, but I'm here to tell you, that's complete bullshit.

Arturo and I were identical physically, but mentally, we were very different. Always had been. When I smiled, he sneered. When I got hurt, he laughed. Ours was a story so opposite of what I was told about twins growing up. We drifted apart very young, joining our own unique friend groups.

Well, I had a friend group. Arturo was a bit of a loner. I told him he needed to treat people better, but he wouldn't listen to me. He had a mean streak which put people off. Maybe he couldn't control it. Some said the easiest way to tell us apart was our eyes. Mine were gentle and kind, and his were...mischievous.

I stare at the crime scene photos, lost in the blood. So much blood. He used a Buck knife. Deborah had one hundred and forty-two stab wounds, my son, Gabriel, had seventy-five stab wounds, and my daughter, Hope, had eighty-two. It is difficult to determine exactly how many were inflicted on each body before death, though many of the lacerations were fatal. But there is evidence he came back and stabbed them all after they were dead. It's amazing what an autopsy can reveal.

Was I supposed to be there? Did he stab them in my absence? Did Arturo intend on killing me too? Would he have inflicted even more stab wounds to my body, getting out all the frustration he harbored and pent up over the years of watching a replica of himself become a happy man in a simple life?

I wasn't successful by any means, or I would have been living in my own damn house rather than a fourplex, but I had something Arturo would never achieve. A family. I was happy, with a future playing out in real time. Deborah and I would grow old together and be blessed with grandchildren.

But Arturo took all of that away.

I often wonder how things would have turned out had I been home. Arturo hadn't been a big a part of my life for many years. We would see one another occasionally at family functions. He became an alcoholic, which made it easy to differentiate us, being he was bloated and overweight.

The last time I saw him it was like looking into one of those mirrors in a funhouse—the ones that distort your reflection. At the time, he watched my family with hawk-like intensity, but I didn't think anything of it. Sure, I recognized jealousy and envy, but never did I think it would manifest into something like 299 stab wounds.

You know what CSI agents say about that many stab wounds, right? It's a crime of passion.

There are sections of the crime reports which are blacked out. I've been told this is for my benefit, despite asking for the reports and photos myself. It was the only stipulation from my contact within the police department. I constantly examine the investigation reports, wondering what was blacked out and why, but I have my assumptions.

My connection won't spill the beans. Supposedly, there are things about the case which are better left unknown to me. He regrets releasing the reports and photos. Had he known it would consume me, he never would have complied with my request.

I don't go into the room where my children were murdered and rarely into the room where Deborah was killed. Now, I sleep on the couch. It's not the same one Arturo offed himself on, but close enough. His body was found on the floor between the couch and coffee table. The original couch was removed due to blood contamination. It was considered hazardous waste. I lie here sometimes, in the exact position his body was found, and ask questions of the dead, to which I never get an answer.

Right now, I'm lying on my side, one arm slumped over my head, though mine is intact whereas Arturo's was a red, wet mess. His brain had oozed out like cranberry sauce. Flaps of hairy skin had been blown back, revealing jagged edges of bloody skull.

"Why?" I ask.

In the crime scene photo, Arturo's body is the same shape as mine. He lost the bloat, shed some pounds. Maybe he planned it this way—coming into the house and convincing my family he was me, catching them unaware. Or maybe his body looks thinner after death.

"Why?" I ask again.

A voice as delicate as fine blown glass says, "Because..."

I close my eyes tight and clench my teeth. Shivers run up and down my body. I taste tequila, even though I haven't had a drink in years. Then I recognize blood.

The voice comes again. "Because we're the same, you and I."

A shiver runs up my body, more fear than chill from the tomb-like cold of the apartment. I leap up from my absurd position on the living room floor and dash across the room. The taste of blood is strong in my mouth. I go into the kitchen and spit in the sink. My saliva is pink. My heart thunders in my chest, and I take a moment to calm myself.

I must have been clenching my teeth, that's all. Or maybe I bit my lip and didn't realize it.

Then comes the gunshot.

**

I crouch as if someone is in the apartment, pointing a gun at me. There is nothing but a ringing in my ears and a terrible headache, which comes on as suddenly as the gunshot. I go back into the living room, smelling cordite. There's a hazy look to the air, like I've been searing a steak over high heat, but I haven't cooked a proper meal in weeks, living off canned goods and frozen dinners.

I never was a very good cook. Deborah was great at it. I miss her food. Miss her and the kids. I have no life without them.

The headache dissipates along with the taste of copper in my mouth and the smell of cordite in the stale air.

I've been told by some I will never get over the massacre of my family. Others say time heals all wounds. I've been advised to get out of my apartment or I'll never move on. But how *can* I? People have a lot to say about things they have no experience with.

Grief is a son of a bitch. No one should have to deal with the pain I deal with. The hurt. The guilt.

I should have been there.

"But you weren't."

The voice speaks into my ear, startling me. I yelp and leap back, my body left with a cold sensation, like a bird freshly plucked of its feathers. The cool air in the stagnant room sweeps over me like a living thing, though there is no window open to allow any such draft.

I swallow hard and clench my eyes closed. The headache begins to resurface, as does the metallic taste in my mouth. When I open my eyes, blood trails down the hallway and streaks on the walls, from hands desperate to escape. My mouth goes dry when the crime scene photos come to life, like absurd visuals from a nightmarish gypsum trip.

The blood looks so real. And then I smell it, heavy in the air.

Strained gasping, like a death rattle, comes from the living room. An inconsistent wheezing drifts through the air, then a wet cough, choking, and more struggled breathing.

In the crime scene photos it is difficult to tell which way the blood smears on the floor are traveling. I assumed, based on the police report, the stains were from my wife and kids when they retreated to their rooms after being attacked. But now, from the blood on the floor around me, it is clear the smeared footprints were from Arturo after he killed them and walked back into the living room.

The wheezing death rattle.

A faint voice chokes out the words, "Goddamn you. Goddamn...your life."

I stand there between the hallway leading to the bedrooms and the living room on the other side of the entry. The blood can't be real, and yet I see it as clear as if I were there when Arturo destroyed my life.

The breathing escalates. I shift my gaze to the living room, to the couch where I sleep every night. It isn't the new couch. There is blood on the headrest and above on the ceiling.

Arturo is dying.

I don't know if I should go to him. Maybe this hallucinatory experience is my twin brother reaching out to make amends. And if it is, do I allow him that forgiveness?

I take a tentative step toward the living room, when crying comes from down the hallway. My heart lurches into my throat, and I hold my breath. I didn't just hear that, did I?

And then it happens again. Soft whimpering. A girl's sniffle and a shushing from a second voice.

My children.

I shake my head and whisper, "Oh God no. Don't do this to me."

In that moment, the world seems to whirl. I become lightheaded, on the verge of fainting. If I drop right now and never wake, I will be okay with that, to spare me the torture playing out all around me—a torment I seem unable to escape.

People have told me I'll go mad living in this apartment. It isn't that I don't believe them. They just don't understand how my heart aches. How the memories of the past seem to fade with each passing day. How difficult it is for me to move on with my life when I want no life other than the one I had. I remain here in this empty tomb to be as close to my family as I can. To try and understand why Arturo did what he did.

I grab one of the crime scene photos from the table and juxtapose it with the apartment. The blood I see is exactly the same, and I wonder if it is tattooed on my mind, forever marring my vision of the place I once called home.

This is no home.

The whimpering stops. The blood evaporates from view. I am back in my apartment.

I haven't had anything like this happen yet. My insistence on remaining here has nothing to do with ghosts. I don't believe in them. The rational part of my brain insists on sleep-deprivation-inspired hallucinations. An overworked mind. Too much time glossing over those grisly photos. An overactive imagination trying too hard to piece things together.

A thump seems to come from the master bedroom, but it might be a neighbor upstairs. When we moved into the fourplex, we were happy to get one of the floor units. Living in such tight quarters with two children is challenging enough without having to worry about bothering the neighbors below with the constant running around and stomping of a couple of youngsters. We also didn't have to worry about them falling out of a window. This is an old building with brittle screens.

Never did I think I was going to have to worry about them being killed by their uncle.

I always had the mindset that no matter how bad the finances are or how tight the budget is, happiness will create good memories children will hold onto for the rest of their lives.

Just so long as they don't know the struggle or have to see it etched upon their parents' faces. They can live in a world painted for them, with bright rainbows and sunshine, and that's exactly how we lived.

Deborah and I agreed to never fight in front of the kids and to always keep them in mind while arguing, which, at times, wasn't easy to do. Living in a small apartment wasn't ideal for a family of four, but they were none the wiser. To them, this was high living. They didn't know any better, and they were happy.

Until the night Arturo stopped by.

I sit on the couch like I imagine he did when he ate the gun and launched his cerebellum onto my ceiling. What must he have thought in that moment, his own mind becoming a splattered mess of bloody chunks? I try to understand why he killed my family.

Over a week ago, I stopped going to work. I just don't see the point anymore. My family was my driving force. I worked for them. Without my wife and kids, what am I? No one from work has called to check in on me. Only management wondering where I am. It's not with sympathy that they call, but pure business. That's okay. In this life, we have nothing if we don't have our family.

*****

Look at the crime scene photos again.
Turn to page 81.

Crawl onto the floor where Arturo died.
Turn to page 124.

I don't know what comes over me, but I cannot help myself. This ethereal being in my apartment intrigues me, no matter how vile his visage. I cross the living room, hardly aware of anything. My vision remains compromised enough, and all I can make out are the faint shapes of things like countertops, cabinets, and furniture.

When I get closer, I notice his flesh is old and dry. His mouth is open. Delicate words come out like brittle parchment.

"I want. To. Touch you."

A shudder runs down my spine. Is coming this close such a good idea? When I close my eyes, that changes nothing. I can still see him. There is nothing in the cavernous sockets of his skeletal face, but something *is* there, pleading and sad.

"Why?"

He makes to answer, but the words don't want to come out. Instead, something dry and crisp, like old leather, protrudes.

His tongue.

I step back, but there isn't far I can go. Something blocks my way. It must be a piece of furniture, but there is nothing behind me.

More of them, all huddled together, blocking my escape. Strange husks of human souls—not quite dead but not alive. They stare at me with those empty eyes and yet, somehow, see me just as clearly as I gaze upon them.

The man who beckons me to the kitchen grabs my arm. I make to pull away, but I cannot. His grip is not so much strong as it is secure, his bony fingers wrapping around my pliable flesh.

Words come out of his cavernous mouth. "Oh, so warm. So, so warm."

The others moan, almost like a chant of ill monks. Soon it turns into words. A legible chant of: *So warm, so warm, so warm.*

The instigator pulls my arm to his face and places it against his clammy, cold skin. I recoil in horror but cannot move.

So warm. So warm. So warm.

The man lifts his other hand, revealing the paring knife. "Your eyes," he says. "Remove them. And be with ussssss." He hangs on that last syllable like a warning—or perhaps an invitation to doom.

I shake my head but utter not a word. For the first time, I understand what people mean by being paralyzed with fear.

"You're so warm," someone says from behind me.

"So, so warm," declares another exasperated voice.

The man shakes his head. It's a sad thing to watch. He is defeated.

Or is he?

The beings grab ahold of me. Their bony digits latch into my body without regard, like dull fragments of stone pushing into my muscle tissue. I struggle, making an attempt to free myself, but their numbers are too large. It seems I am stuck.

The eerie man before me uses the paring knife on my arm, cutting around my bicep. I plead and struggle, but they have me good. He then slices straight down the length of my arm to the palm of my hand. It's a simple cut which causes blood to weep and trickle, dripping onto the kitchen floor.

The pain isn't all that bad, but the agony of the situation has me reeling. Yet there's nothing I can do. He then hands the knife to some yearning skeletal hand reaching out from behind me.

Having lost sight of the knife fills me with dread. The man before me grabs the edges of my flesh, where he made his cuts, and digs his dried fingers in, pulling like skinning an animal. That's when real pain erupts.

I scream and shudder and flail. He pulls from my shoulder, yanking down in jerky motions. My flesh frees itself from the muscle beneath. I don't know what feels worse—the flesh ripping or the air on exposed muscle tissue.

Soon enough, he removes the skin from my arm and hand in one long, fleshy glove fit for Ed Gein.

I watch through tears while he puts on the skin, wrapping it around his corpse-like arm. The blood and fatty tissue cling to his dried flesh, strangely form-fitting. His odd mouth dips into a smile. The vacant, milky orbs in his deep-set eye sockets roll back in great pleasure.

The others become excited, grabbing at my raw arm and rubbing their cold flesh against my warm, running blood. Their cold is strangely soothing on my bare flesh, and yet there is nothing that can conqueror the pain in that moment.

They strip me of my clothes, and the paring knife goes to work again, passed from hand to hand. Limb by limb, they cut away my flesh, leaving me exposed and hurting, like some morbid anatomy lesson. They put the new skin over their cold, dead bodies and have a moment of happiness.

While I fade away, sweet death calls me to an eternity I can only hope isn't a fraction of the hell these poor souls are trapped in. I watch the one who initially beckoned me to the kitchen.

He stares at his arms in sadness. The warmth of my flesh is now chilled and useless.

***

The correct choice was Turn away from the stranger.
Turn to page 90.

When the mop leaves Danny's grasp, I seize my opportunity and leap for it, grabbing the handle before it hits the ground. Jan is already in motion, with the cleaver raised. She brings the sharpened steel down into Danny's face.

In that intense moment, he turns, catching the blade through his cheek and temple, but the weapon has no trouble breaking through skull. He goes down hard, though the cleaver doesn't become embedded.

Jan dives for her precious hunk of steel at the same moment I slap her across the cheek with the blood-soaked mop head. The effect isn't quite what I desire, but it's better than nothing. I hit her again, whipping the saturated mop fibers like a cat o' nine tails. Jan screeches and puts her hands up to shield her face.

I bring the mop down again in a quick motion, only this time, she catches it. Her sharp reflexes startle me, reminding me I'm dealing with an Olympian. She grips the mop head tight and yanks. I'm pulled off-balance but manage to maintain my position, struggling in a bizarre game of tug-of-war.

From the corner of my eye, I notice Danny twitching on the floor, his body wracked with a series of spasms. All it takes is that moment of distraction for Jan to pull on the gory mop head even harder and launch me down at her feet. She kicks me in the face.

Apparently, not only was Jan a champion runner at one time, but she still does it for fun and exercise. Her kick is like that of a kangaroo. I yelp and let go of the mop handle. My hands come up defensively to my face in a reaction I can't control.

Jan rears back. She breathes heavy and deep. Maybe she's wearing out. My face throbs where she kicked me, my right eye swelling closed. My cheek is wet from blood where her shoe ripped the flesh. I stand, but my equilibrium is off.

When I stumble, Jan retreats into the living room. I go after her, bracing myself on the backs of furniture. My hands leave bloody prints she'll surely bitch about having to clean before her Bunco game.

Before I know it, a crazed look masks her face. Her teeth are bared and gritted, like a junkyard dog on an intruder. By the time I notice she's hefting one of those massive three-wick Yankee candles in a thick glass jar, it is being thrust at me. I try to duck, but the damn thing ricochets off my temple, causing a pain to match her kick. This is what she needs. I'm stunned.

My vision is stunted by half, and I'm teetering around like a goddamned drunk. I make my way through the living room.

How the hell did things get to this point? How the hell can an old woman subdue me like this? If I make it out of this situation alive, how can I even attempt to recount the details of this struggle without eliciting laughter from anyone I dare tell the story to?

But alas, that isn't my fate in this age-defying battle. Jan has one up on me.

When she turns with the ash shovel from the fireplace, I'm thankful it's not the poker. But that relief is short-lived when Jan rushes me. I put my arms up to deflect her onslaught, only to have my wrists hacked up by the sharp metal edge.

She jabs at my arms in quick bursts. The razor-sharp edge lacerates my flesh and clangs against the bone. Blood flies everywhere. Chunks of muscle dangle from my arms like renegade bark flaking off a eucalyptus tree. I scream.

When I remove my hands to free them of her torments, the ash shovel is lodged into my neck.

I wheeze and gasp for air, managing nothing but bloody squeaks. My shoulder catches on the arm of her couch as I fall to the floor. The ash shovel is tossed to the side.

I still can't breathe properly. Blood fills my throat, and I choke on it while Jan stands above, watching and shaking her head. My mother looked at me like that when I was a kid and did something wrong. For some reason, I feel ashamed.

"All I wanted was help cleaning the place up before Bunco. Was that too much to ask?"

***

Try again. Turn to page 51.

***

"You want to use a piece of my finger to cook with? Isn't that...morbid?"

"Not morbid, Gary. Tasty. Why don't you lick your finger and see for yourself?"

I regard her like a car salesman and ponder her suggestion, scrolling through the negative results in my mind. It's clear I'm changing into produce, but why? What if my body *can* be used to cook food? What then? Will I be plucked one piece at a time until there is nothing left?

I bring my hand to my mouth and stick out my tongue, placing the tip on the area she dug her nail into. Indeed, it tastes like ginger. I'm shocked and appalled at this revelation.

"So how about it?" she says.

The look in her eyes has me on edge. Her callous disregard for the strange state I find myself in is unsettling.

"Just a piece," I say. "What if I change back and what you've taken from me is actually flesh?"

Tanya reaches out an eager hand and grabs the light caramel-colored end of my thumb. She makes a quick gesture, snapping off the tip. I recoil, though there is no pain.

"It's a risk I'm willing to take," she says.

After she leaves, I stare at my hand, fingers splayed. The tip of the thumb is gone. I'm left with a flat edge smelling heavily of fresh ginger, which reminds me of my grandmother's kitchen. Memories of my visits there flood my mind.

I stare at my broken thumb. What will become of me if she carries on like this, taking bits and pieces until there is nothing left of me? What will happen if I suddenly return to my natural state? Will my thumb hurt? Will it bleed? Would Tanya finally take me to the ER?

On my side of the bed, in the nightstand, I keep a knife. A pocketknife. I lean over and reach my good hand for the drawer. The knife is a nice one with an ivory inlaid handle, handed down to me by my grandfather. I keep the blade sharp but use it mostly to open mail. It's not much of a safety device and wouldn't do me any good against a gun, but there's something comforting about having it.

I open the blade and eye the gleaming edge. When I glide it over my malformed thumb, it slices off a good chunk. The air around me is enveloped in the sweet, pungent aroma of ginger. Grandpa's blade and Grandma's ginger. I cut again, taking another section, almost down to my palm.

The pale color of ginger turns fleshy.

I hack even more, and this time I feel pain.

The faint yellow core of fragrant root is now a weeping sore dripping blood on Tanya's freshly laundered sheets. But I don't care. I cut off my other fingers right down to the nubs, where I begin to bleed. The pain shoots up my arm, but it's something I can understand. I *should* feel pain.

After removing my foot from beneath the covers, I use the knife to whack away my potato toes. Only this time, I do it in a frenzy. The fingerlings shoot off in all directions, bouncing on the hardwood. Soon enough, I hit meat. I continue to cut and slice, gritting my teeth against the pain.

I am real. Not a fucking sack of produce.

Real.

"What's going on in here?" Tanya comes through the doorway. Her mouth and eyes open wide when she sees the blood on our stark white sheets.

"Gary, what are you doing?"

"I'm real, Tanya. *Real!*"

I drag Grandpa's blade across my neck. It digs deep enough to slice through my trachea, and I struggle to breathe, choking on blood.

Tanya screams.

I laugh and gurgle and laugh and gurgle and laugh and gurgle and...

***

The correct choice was Deny her request to use ginger finger for cooking. Turn to page 20.

We pause. Jan's words ring in our heads. Dan grabs the front door handle, eager to be out of here, and I cannot blame him. Things are getting too weird too quickly.

He tries to turn it, but it's locked. Dan shakes it more vigorously, but it won't budge. That's about the time the axe catches him in the back of the neck.

The sound of his body slamming against the door is much louder than the axe embedding itself where his spine connects to his head. On the other side of the door is a slender stairwell leading down to the little lobby of the building. His body thudding against the wood so suddenly causes a crashing boom to echo through that stairwell, like an alarm bell to alert the other tenants.

Well, those who aren't at work in the middle of the day.

I turn just as Jan lets go of the axe. She takes a few paces back, allowing Dan's body to collapse onto the floor, where he twitches and convulses. I give her a wary look, then crouch, as if I can do something to help Dan. But a wound like that seems fatal.

He shakes like he's lying naked on a frozen lake. His eyes stare into mine. He's conscious of what's happening, even though he cannot properly communicate.

"It's okay, Dan," I say. I don't even know why. It certainly is *not* going to fucking be okay.

He tries to say something and chokes on blood.

"*Shhhh*. Just close your eyes."

He does.

"What the fuck is wrong with you?" I ask, watching my employee and friend die.

"Me?" The incredulous nature of her voice is more shocking than it really should be at this point. "You can't just walk out on me like that. I *hired* you for a job."

I stand and turn toward her. As a bald man with a tight beard and a scar on the side of my head, I know how intimidating

I appear when I glare at her. It's a look I only use in situations that call for it. Otherwise, I am as gentle as an orchid.

"Our job isn't to clean *active* crime scenes. You killed your fucking husband! You can't just call a cleaning service to remove the body. That's a crime, don't you see? I should be calling the—"

I stop myself right there. Jan's eyes pop wide. She expects me to tell her who I should be calling. That probably would be a good enough reason for her to give me the same treatment as Thomas and Dan, which would result in me assaulting an elderly woman. And I'd probably get convicted for killing all of them. No one would believe she did this.

"I don't have time to call anybody else to do this for me," Jan says in a sweet older woman's voice, which does not, in any shape or form, fit this wild scenario. "That is, if I have to kill you too. So I suggest you start cleaning this mess up. It would have been easier with the two of you. Now you have twice as much to take care of."

"I don't have shit to take care of." I pull out my phone. "I'm calling the police. This has gone way too fucking far."

In that moment, she shows me how agile she is by leaping across the room and yanking the embedded cleaver from her husband's body. It makes a sucking noise when it is removed from his gut.

I fumble with my phone, trying to open the screen with my fingerprint. It isn't working. I try to unlock it with my passcode, but I must have hit the wrong number with one of my fat digits. She swings the cleaver down when I go for the door handle, lopping off my other hand, right along with my cell phone.

The cleanness of the cut attests for a honed edge on the blade. I don't feel a thing until I bring my stump around to assist my other hand, which futilely jiggles the front doorknob. All I do is smear crimson all over the door. That's when I feel the pain.

Blood spurts out with every beat of my heart. Pain shoots up that arm. I turn and squirt blood right into her face. Jan screams.

She slips on the bloody hardwood but manages to grab the hilt of the axe embedded in Dan's neck. Jan yanks it out and hefts it above her head.

"Goddamn you!" she yells. "I just wanted my house cleaned!"

The blade swings into my face at a speed I cannot avoid. With a loud thump, everything goes black.

***

The correct choice was Turn around and try to communicate with her. Turn to page 43.

At some point, I crawl onto the floor, mimicking the position Arturo was found in. I fall asleep like this for many nights, hoping to dream something that will give me closure.

When I wake, my head is throbbing. I move, hearing a squelching sound.

The heavy copper odor of blood enters my nostrils like a foul perfume. I move against a sickening pull, as if my head is somehow fused to the carpet. A slight panic takes hold, and I move more briskly, removing my face from its suction to the carpet. It's like my scalp is being peeled from my head.

From a crouching position, I can now see the blood. It's everywhere. The pool in which I lie has dark fragments: chunks of brain, skull bits, and coagulated blood. The seal around it ripped when I removed my head from the very spot where Arturo bled out onto the floor.

I place a hand to my head, caressing the concave wound and the sticky mush of obliterated brain. Wet tendrils of hair dangle at the edges of my fractured skull, thick with drying blood.

Or is it Arturo's skull?

How can it be me? I didn't die that night. It was Arturo.

My head aches like someone is beating on it with a hammer, right at the point where the bullet exited, blowing half my, er, *Arturo's* head skyward. My tongue probes the roof of my mouth and the indention where the bullet entered. I shudder at the strangeness of it all, the stark reality of such a thing.

Is this a lucid dream, a fold in reality, or some kind of sick nightmare I am being forced to endure? Is this what I've been waiting for?

A deafening blast echoes in my mind, startling me. My head makes an involuntary jerking motion. Blood runs down my back in a sudden warm flow, and yet my body erupts in gooseflesh from it trickling between my shoulder blades. I taste copper, choking on the blood running down my throat.

Another deafening blast, as if an M80 has exploded inside my skull. A wedge has been hammered into my head, and the offender is twisting and prying my skull apart, attempting to gain access to my brain.

I clasp hands over my face and scream through gritted teeth. And then it's gone.

The room is as it has been since after the crime scene clean-up crew removed the biohazard—the blood of my family.

It's sometime in the middle of the night. The witching hour, as it were. Everything is still. Moonlight filters in through the blinds. Shadows hide nothing, for everything is out in the open. There's nothing darkness can conceal from me in this lingering memory of the worst night of my life. No idle childhood fear can begin to rise above what I wallow in daily.

After the apartment was cleaned and everything removed—including mattresses, throw rugs, the couch, anything that had been touched with blood or other human remains—I was ushered back in as if nothing had happened. As if the torment of living amongst the ethereal fibers of my departed ones would not have an adverse effect on my mental health.

If it was a house I owned, I could have sold it. But to be honest, I don't think I would have done anything differently.

Guilt is a vicious beast of burden.

The spot on the floor at the foot of my new couch, where Arturo was found, left quite a stain. The owner of the building, a man who lives up on a hill overlooking Greenwood Planes—like Norman Bates's house overlooked the motel—will have to have the floors refinished to remove it. He won't dare do something like that while a tenant is living here, though. The cheap bastard.

I lie on the floor in the very position Arturo was photographed in when the police documented the scene. Every night, I do this. And every day. I do this because I have nothing to live for. Because I want answers I can never have.

In that lucid state between reality and dreams, I feel something beneath me. I close my eyes and imagine the worst things a husband and father could think of. What was it like when Arturo killed my family? Not in a fantasy sort of way, but in cold, hard reality. I imagine what their last thoughts were. Their terror.

And the feeling of something beneath me intensifies. Tiny tendrils reach from the weathered and blood-soaked floorboards, etching into my body, like threads being woven into my flesh. It's painful, but not nearly as much as the memories of that night. Whatever my family endured at the hands of my bastard twin was so much worse.

Agony, like fingers pushing through my muscle, causes me to stiffen with a gasp. I try to move, but I am tethered. A noise disrupts the silence of the room—the leathery sounds of whatever oozes from the floor into my skin. My eyes shoot open.

Footsteps approach from behind. I twist my head as much as I can from the bonds holding me firmly and see myself towering over the couch.

Is it me, or is it Arturo?

"Come with me," the man who looks like me says.

I'm filled with a sudden and irrevocable dread. The substance holding my body in place is like acid on my skin. My breathing accelerates into hyperventilation, chest heaving in and out. I think I'm going to pass out.

In that very moment, when the lights are dimming, my consciousness escapes my body in something as close to astral projection as I can imagine. I drift toward the man who looks exactly like me. It's more of a feeling than anything else. And then we collide. My consciousness blends with the physical manifestation of the man who wrought an early demise of my hopes and dreams.

His heartbeat accelerates the blood in his veins. I feel like myself, and yet there is something different—a darkness in my mind I have never felt before. Like an ink spot covering my normal thoughts, rendering them useless as memories, as if everything meant nothing. I've never experienced so much darkness in my life, so much coldness.

After several minutes of grasping my bearings, I begin to feel as if I'm merely losing my mind, drifting back into one of the hallucinatory trips I have been manifesting recently.

But no...Something is different this time. My body is still on the ground where Arturo died. It is fused to the floor by thin fingers of gore seeping from between the floorboards and embedding into my flesh. I stare at myself, into my own eyes, and I don't know who I am anymore.

The room is as it was the day everything went to shit. The tiny bloody footprints and red smears on the walls. The splatter on the ceiling, dripping like chunky spaghetti sauce. A haze hangs in the air from the gunshot.

"They tried to get away," I say, only it isn't what I'm thinking. It is Arturo's voice, but it sounds just like me.

Did our voices always sound so similar?

I take slow steps forward and make it to the hallway. But I'm careful not to step in any of the blood, as if by doing so I am tampering with a crime scene. That is exactly how I see the house: one big crime scene.

"It's not a crime scene yet." Arturo's voice comes from my mouth. Or is his voice coming from *his* mouth?

Confusion grips me, but I pad forward down the hall, unable to keep from stepping in fresh, wet drips of blood. Both bedroom doors are closed. Muffled sounds of crying come from my children's room. Deborah must be doing a better job of keeping quiet.

*****

Do not go into either door. Turn to page 133.

Open the door on the right. Turn to page 75.

Open the door on the left. Turn to page 54.

I shift my gaze skyward and look through the window at the glowing sun being covered by the dark circle of a full moon. It's absolutely breathtaking. The ZZ Top soundtrack in my mind is remedied with Pink Floyd, and all is forgotten for that moment. There is no pain in my retinas, which encourages the hope that staring into the eclipse isn't as dangerous as I've been told.

The sky darkens, and it's as if the world is transported to nighttime in the middle of the day. Through the window come the *oohs* and *aahs* of the people below.

I stare into the eclipse, even though it is bad for my eyes, but I don't care anymore. There is no pain. I know what I am doing is wrong. I just. Don't. Care.

With the darkness comes a sensation of bitter cold, which I mistake for a drastic change in temperature due to the vacancy of the sun. But it's just *them* crowding closer, as if they want to have a look too. Their presence is similar to a giant freezer behind me, the door wide open. I shiver when the brightness of the halo in the sky burns into my mind—a searing poker branding my brain with its brilliance.

With somnambulist intensity, I stare as if nothing around me matters. Not the chill of death pressing upon me. Not the fleeting memories of Amy. Not the fact I am doing irreparable damage to my eyes. Nothing matters in this moment. If I could, I would walk through the window and swim to the halo burning bright in the darkened sky. Drift upward and fade away into nothing.

But I cannot do that, and soon the moon shifts across the sun. The darkness begins its retreat from a unique midday spectacle. Only I am left staring endlessly at the crescent sun revealed to me from behind the passing moon.

I feel the pain now. It hurts to look at, but I remain stoic. This is better than what I have been dealing with. Better than remembering what can never be. Better than *them* staring at me expectantly.

My head throbs. The moon has now freed the sun to shine its brilliance onto the world. Everything becomes an oversaturated bright white, with dancing halos of green and blue. The lingering afterimage of the eclipse dances through a world of nothing. I push myself against the window.

When I moved into this apartment, I thought the windows were so old and thin they would shatter easily. Now I pound on one, but it doesn't break. It's like I'm slamming my fists against Plexiglas. I cannot see, but I know there are people below, those who set up lawn chairs to watch the eclipse. Do they see me? Will one of them try to help?

Finally, I give up my futile attempt at gaining their attention and stand there, staring into the great bright nothing. The afterimages have since faded, and with it, my vision has abandoned me. With the loss of my sight, their hands are on me even stronger than before. They begin to grip and pull. At first, I stand determined, tethering myself to that position before the window, but their energy is greater than it has ever been.

I am uncertain whether to lose the battle or allow them to take me, so I fight it. My body is wrenched backward, and I am flung to the floor. Though my vision has been reduced to the ever-present moment of a flashbulb going on before an old-fashioned photograph, I see *them* all around me. They leap upon my body like eager nymphs, nuzzling close and moaning in some bizarre ecstasy not carnal in nature.

A mouth closes on my wrist, and that is when I am certain they are vampires. Then the bite that seals my assumption. But no...the people of the light do not drink my blood. They smear their faces in it.

"Oh, so warm," one of them says.

"Give *me* the warmth." Another snatches my bleeding hand away.

Teeth rip a hole in my other wrist. I wince from the pain but manage well enough, ready for this all to be over with. My wrists are on fire, but shock and my inability to see dull the wrenching agony.

A mouth lingers at my throat. Instinct causes me to move my head around, as if to stop the inevitable from happening, but I fight my natural inclinations. Teeth bear down on my throat and tear. This is a pain I cannot stand.

I thrash around, but they have me pinned tight. They marvel at the gushes of blood shooting from my carotid artery. The last thing I hear while I fade away is a low grumbling laughter, like elderly children.

***

Try again. Turn to page 97.

I try the door on the left. It opens to a pristine room, this one clearly the master bedroom. The bed is made with sharp lines and not a wrinkle in sight. The dresser looks to be about thirty years old, yet just as spotless and clean as the day it left the manufacturer. On top is a framed wedding photo, faded with age, along with a wallet and keys.

The room is perfect—the pictures on the walls symmetrical, the mirror over the vanity spotless.

I wonder why she snapped. Surely, Thomas was the same person this morning he has been for all these years they've been married. What did he do that caused her to—

The thumping of footsteps from behind breaks my thoughts.

Jan runs down the hallway at a ridiculous speed, considering her age. She has used apron strings to securely tighten an oven mitt over her throat. But that's about all I can see before she swings the solid wood rolling pin into my face.

It happens so quickly, there is no way for me to even attempt blocking the damaging blow. I go flying backward into the bedroom. Jan's momentum causes her to go down with me. I grab her throat, hoping I have the upper ground, when I hear a whirring sound.

The crazy old bitch grabbed a cordless electric knife from the kitchen!

She drags it over my wrists, raggedly severing the veins and causing me to pull my hands away from her throat. Blood pours down my arms like a suicide, but death isn't instant, even when the wounds are mortal in nature. That's why I feel it when she drags the whirring knife across my neck.

The sound it makes while it tears through my trachea is like cutting through cooked turkey bones and tough gristle. Blood spurts onto her wrinkled cheeks and drips off like juice from a ripe pomegranate.

***

The correct choice was Take the door on the right.
Turn to page 65.

The cries of my family are fearful and uncertain, gradually descending into pain and suffering, as if being slowly dipped into a pot of boiling water. I close my eyes to block out the sound, but all I can see are the grisly crime scene photos, police reports, and the images my mind created to fill in the blanks. My contact blacking out material he thought was too heavy for me did nothing more than cause me to imagine terrible things, perhaps worse than what actually happened.

Deborah's whimpers escalate, and though my instinct is to burst through the door, there is nothing I can do to change the past. What's done is done. She's dead. Hope is dead. Gabriel is dead.

And I was at the bar when they were murdered.

Like a brat who didn't get his way, I was angry with Deborah for something so inconsequential. I left her here with the kids, knowing she couldn't come after me if she wanted to, that she was stuck until I decided to return. I went to Cheers N Beers and put down a few brews with people I convinced myself were friends, talking shit and complaining about my wife, while she and my children were delivered 299 stab wounds.

There is no reason for me to torture myself like this, to wallow in the pain and tragedy of the past. I fight with the possibility of what might have happened. For one, I wouldn't have let the bastard in to begin with. The reality that I was the one who left the door unlocked, leaving in a fit the way I did that evening, is something I also struggle with. I could blame maintenance for not repairing the lock to the lobby, but I only have myself to blame for not being there in the first place.

"You could have done a lot to prevent what happened."

The voice comes from the living room. It is similar to mine but with a sinister bend to it. It's Arturo. Another one of my hallucinatory trips. A man watching himself go insane.

"No, it's not. It's me. Arturo."

Down the hall, he rises from between the couch and the coffee table. His face is bloody, flaps of his head dangling like morbid party favors. His mouth is crooked, teeth missing. He stares at me from across the expanse of the apartment. I cannot tell if this is some twist of reality or my mind playing more tricks on me.

"It's me," Arturo says. "I'm here."

"Why?" I ask him, as I have every night since the tragedy. "Why?"

"You could have done more to prevent this."

I shake my head. "How?"

"You could have been my brother."

"But I *am* your brother—"

"A *better* brother."

I take a few steps forward. "You kind of made that hard, you know?"

"No one's perfect. So, I had some problems. So what? All my life, I was shit on while you were given praise. I was ignored while you were showered with gifts. I was abandoned while your life flourished. I had shit, and you had everything." Arturo chuckles, the phlegm in his throat—or perhaps blood—bubbling. "*Had.* That's the operative word, isn't it?"

"So you think you can just come into my life and take everything away from me?"

After a pause of consideration, Arturo responds. "I did, didn't I? Your kids thought I was you. Isn't that funny? They thought Daddy was hurting them."

Anger rises within. I take a few more steps toward the visage of my bastard brother.

"I killed them slowly," he says. "They hurt plenty. Then I went to your beautiful wife. I convinced her the kids were still alive. I told her that she needed to fuck me like I was you. I even had her call me by *your* name while I was fucking her. I shoved it down her throat until she choked and pulled it out just in time so she could breathe. When she struggled, I told her I would kill your kids. But I'd already killed them." Arturo shakes his head, smirking. "I was kind of hoping you'd come home and find us like that, but you never showed up. I killed her with the knife, then I sat in the living room, waiting for you."

I come closer and realize I have grabbed a knife.

"I waited for you for what seemed like hours," Arturo continues. "I sat here on the couch. Then I got antsy and returned to the rooms where your dead family lay, getting cold. I stabbed them more, imagining it was you. I kind of lost my mind. It got me hard, so I started fucking the wounds, cutting bigger holes and fucking your family. It was my way of saying 'fuck you' to the twin who abandoned me when he could have done something to help, could have shown some compassion."

I'm close enough to touch him. There's something in his eyes. Sadness and tears are welling there.

"Don't you understand?" he asked. "When someone says bad things about another person enough, everyone starts to believe it. Mom and Dad favored you, so you were blind to their abuse of me, but the effect was that you believed their bullshit. All I needed was some help, someone to be there for me. We're connected by more than blood. We share the same genes. If anyone in this world could have helped me, it was you. But you decided to leave me behind, as if I was a shit smear on a piece of toilet paper to be flushed into the sewer. I called, but you were always brief, irritated. I could tell. Do you remember that? Me calling you?"

I nod. "I was...busy."

"Too busy for the man who once shared a womb? That's fucked up."

"You didn't have to do what you did."

"Maybe I was stopping by to talk to you and I snapped. Maybe I just wanted someone to be there for *me* for a change."

While I can't explain it, feelings of regret and sorrow come over me, despite what Arturo did to my family. I want to understand, and though his reasons aren't enough to justify his actions, I gain the closure I have been seeking all these months in this desolate tomb.

"I know you can't forgive me," he says, his voice cracking. "But please forgive the boy who spent Christmases with you. The boy who shared birthdays with you. The boy who shared a crib. A womb."

Something inside hitches, and a shiver runs through my body. Arturo reaches his arms out, and I accept his embrace, remembering where we came from. Despite how much we've grown apart, we are still twins. We share a deeper connection than most siblings.

I shudder as I pull the knife up and slam it into Arturo's back

. . .

Only, he isn't really there.

I plunge the knife into my own chest, and the blade sticks deep, slipping between ribs and embedding in the meat.

Arturo laughs. "You stupid fuck. You're such a weasel. You weren't there, but I knew I could get you somehow. I didn't come to talk or ask for forgiveness. I came to take what you have, and I fuckin' did it, bro. I fuckin' did it."

I stumble away from the living room. The horrific images of a murder house flash in and out of reality. One second, the floor is covered with bloody footprints, and the next, thick layers of dust coat the paths I tread through. I look back into the living room. Arturo is smiling, his face bloody, the flap of skin hanging from the exit wound. The image of Arturo flickers but remains.

I stagger into the little alcove dining area just off the kitchen, where the police reports and crime scene photos are scattered across the table. My dirty obsession, like a constant reminder of the worst thing I will ever go through. I have breathed and slept my family's murders. Have allowed it to consume me.

Blood soaks my shirt. The knife remains, protruding from my chest. I don't want to remove it for fear it will cause further damage.

There is one thing I must do. I collect the photos and reports from the table and bring them into the kitchen. When I pass the doorway leading into the foyer and living room, I notice Arturo flickering like poor reception on an old TV. He glares at me but says nothing.

In the kitchen, I place the papers and photos in the sink. From beneath it, I procure a small container of Zippo lighter fluid and douse everything. I grab a small box of wood matches, light one, and drop it onto the pile.

As the final shreds of my horrible obsession burn, I remove the knife from my chest. Blood pours out of the wound in a torrent. With a jolt of pain, I stagger back into the living room. Black smoke rises from the sink.

I lie down on the floor, at rest with my twin, as we once were in the womb.

Try Not to Die in This Damned House V

"Fuck, *fuck*, FUCK!" Markus yelled, fleeing the room.

Deanna continued to beat the shit out of the fetus in her womb. He cried and sobbed while she did so.

Markus returned moments later with a paring knife.

"You dumb-ass, stupid bitch." He approached Deanna. "I should have known better than to use you, you fucking drunk."

"I had a life! You took everything from me. You...You..." She shook her head. Tears ran rivulets down her dirty face, making clean paths through the grime. They dripped off her chin onto her bare breasts and misshapen stomach.

"You had *nothing*. I saw you. I watched you with my telescope. I saw you get that bottle every other day. What did you do with it? I *saw* you wasting your life away, just like my mother. I saw you and knew you were the one. I needed you to make a baby for me. To give your life meaning."

"Fuck you!" She punctuated her curse with a massive punch to her belly, which caused her to wince.

"Stop, goddamn it!"

Markus crouched in the blood at Deanna's outstretched legs. He looked between her thighs and saw nothing but red.

"Is the baby coming?" he asked.

Through heavy breaths, she said, "The baby. Is dead."

Markus shifted his gaze to look her in the eyes. His chin trembled, and he shook his head. "No. No, it can't be."

Deanna managed to smile while she nodded. A crazed woman with a dirty face and tangled hair. Her limbs were skin and bone, which caused her belly to have the appearance of being more protrusive than it was—now battered and turning black and blue.

"Goddamn you!"

Markus knelt again in the blood. He used his free hand and planted his palm on Deanna's chest, pushing her. She was too weak to fight. Her body fell backward.

He placed the paring knife at the top of her swollen vagina and cut through her clit in an upward motion, separating flesh like fileting a fish. She screamed when he drew the blade over the curvature of her belly, only managing to bite through the muscle rather than her womb. Markus traced the same path, this time applying more pressure.

The knife split open the uterus, revealing a bloody mess. He thrust his hands into the gore, grasping the tiny fetus, and pulled it free. The umbilical cord was the only lingering attachment to Momma.

It sat in his hands, unmoving, like a fleshy rubber doll.

Markus shook his head. "No. No, it can't be. It just can't be."

He jiggled the fetus, but it didn't move. Deanna's body laid still, her head tilted to the side, eyes staring straight ahead.

Markus looked upon the stillborn body of his heir with sad eyes. Everything he had dreamed of over the past nine months had been washed away by the selfish acts of another alcoholic, there to fuck things up and cause him irreparable damage. Just like his parents.

Once he collected himself and calmed a bit, he took his stillborn child and placed it into a gallon-sized pickle jar. He poured rubbing alcohol over it as a preservative. In the attic, he placed the jar upon an altar-like table near the massive model of the town in the valley below.

"Son," Markus began, "let me tell you about this special place your great-great-grandfather created called Greenwood Planes."

THE END

For more of Markus and his models, check out

This Damned House

and

This Damned House II

For more fun-filled deaths, please check out the rest of the
Try Not to Die series.
Available on Amazon

How Did You Do?

We hope you enjoyed the book and wouldn't mind giving us a little feedback. Thank you so much for your support.

Scan below to answer a few questions about your reading experience.

Thanks

I would like to thank those of you who have read and supported my *This Damned House* books. Being able to bring another quadplex of madness into the *Try Not to Die* series was quite a fun challenge. I hope you had as good a time reading this book as I did writing it.

About the Author

Robert Essig is the author of 22 books including *Baby Fights*, *This Damned House*, *Broth House*, and *Master of Bodies*. He has published over 100 short stories and edited three anthologies. His anthology *Chew On This!* was nominated for a Splatterpunk Award. Robert lives with his family in East Tennessee.

To follow Robert and visit his store, go to:
https://linktr.ee/robertessig

Download Your Free Copy

Includes the first two chapters and one death scene from each of the first seven books in the *Try Not to Die* series. Also look for the second sampler which includes books 8-14.